HARD TARGET

HARD TARGET

THE SILENCER SERIES BOOK 3

MIKE RYAN

WWW.MIKERYANBOOKS.COM

Cover Design: The Cover Collection

Edited By: Graham Toseland

1

It'd been three months since the day Recker found the body of Susan Hanley, stuffed in the trunk of her Honda Civic. Against his better judgment, he never sought revenge or retribution for the killing of Mia's friend. Though he disagreed with the professor's feelings, he nevertheless went along with Jones' desires. Recker pledged that if the police hadn't solved the murder and arrested the culprit by this time, that he'd get back on the case to do his own justice. Unfortunately for him, his own cases seemed to be never ending and he couldn't get back to the investigation of Hanley's murder. In the last couple of months, Recker never even had more than one day off to just relax, let alone the time he'd need to look into the Hanley case.

Though he didn't know the Hanley woman personally, with her being a friend of Mia's, it ate away at Recker that a killer was out there on the loose. Mia asked him constantly if he had the time to work on her friend's death. Over the past three months, she had become increasingly frustrated over the lack of police progress on the situation. Every time she called the police to speak to the investigators, she felt like they were giving her the runaround. She felt that they were nowhere near solving the case and she was sure they were not even investigating it any more. They didn't seem to have any leads, and she wondered if they'd just moved on to other cases that they felt were more solvable. Even though she had pestered Recker at least three times a week to enquire about Hanley's case, he tried not to get too annoyed by it, even though it sometimes took his focus off the cases he was working on now. He understood how frustrated she'd become. He felt it too.

Sitting in the diner of Joe's, one of their frequent meeting places, Recker could only assume that the Hanley case would be one of the first things that Mia brought up. Though she hadn't mentioned it the day before when she asked him to meet her for lunch, he figured he was going to hear questions about it today. Since she was running a few minutes late due to traffic, she'd already texted him to let him know she'd be there soon. Sitting there by himself, though, gave Recker some time to himself to think. With all the cases he'd been working lately and how busy he was, just taking a few minutes to think was something he didn't get much time to do.

Recker looked out the window and watched a younger couple getting into their car. For some reason; possibly the woman's blonde hair that bore a striking resemblance to Carrie's, his thoughts turned back to her. He thought about a few of the good times that they'd shared together. But those thoughts quickly turned darker when he thought about that fateful night back in London. He replayed the conversation he had with Agent 17 in his mind, over and over again. Though he was looking out the window, he wasn't seeing anything. In his mind, he was picturing what Agent 17 looked like as he had that conversation over the phone. Recker clenched his jaw tighter as his body embraced the tension that was flowing through him. Then, the image he had of Agent 17 slowly faded away as Recker's mind turned to other things. He thought about the professor's software program that was supposed to be helping find and identify Carrie's killer. With how busy they'd become, Recker had put the search out of his mind as he focused on helping the people in the city he was now in. But as he sat there thinking about it, he was becoming more agitated at the fact that Jones still hadn't found Agent 17 yet. Of course, the professor could have found him already, and he just didn't want to reveal it to Recker yet with the amount of cases they had on the table. But Recker also knew that Jones was reluctant to participate in the search, anyway. He was starting to think that unless he pestered Jones continuously about it, that the professor would never make it a priority. Jones would always find a way to put it on the back burner if Recker let him. Recker thought about the last time he asked about how the search was going. It'd probably been about a month, and it was only in passing as they were in the middle of another kidnapping case. He remembered Jones not saying much about it, just indicating that they were close.

As he sat there thinking about it, he determined that when lunch with Mia was done, he was going back to the office to confront Jones about his lack of haste in finding what was so important to Recker. He would accept no excuses or delays, and he wasn't going to take no for an answer. After all, finding Agent 17 was one of the conditions Recker insisted on when he agreed to join Jones' crusade. If he didn't like Jones' answer, then Recker would seriously consider leaving on the spot to go find the one person on earth that he hated like no other.

Recker was so deep in thought that he never even saw or heard Mia sit down across from him. She hurriedly rushed into the diner and sat down, knowing that Recker usually didn't have an overabundance of time on his hands. Once she settled in, she sighed and looked at him, noticing that he was obviously somewhere else since he didn't pay her even the slightest bit of attention. Seeing that he was looking out the window, Mia glanced out herself, wondering if something was going on out there. Not noticing anything strange, she looked back at him, curious as to what was going through that mind of his. In the time that they'd known each other, she noticed that he sometimes seemed to get lost in another moment and she often wondered just where exactly his mind went. Mia cleared her throat, hoping the noise would awaken him from whatever trance he was in, but he still paid her no mind. Though part of her wasn't sure whether she should wake him, as part of her worried that in these moments of his, he was taken back to some violent moment in his life. Seeing Recker's hand resting on the table, she reached her hand across and gently placed it on top of his. Feeling her touch, his concentration was broken, and he turned to look at her, somewhat surprised to see her sitting there.

"Hey, when'd you get here?" he asked.

"Oh, like an hour ago," Mia teased.

"Really?"

"No. I just got here a minute ago."

"Oh. I didn't even notice you come in."

"Yeah, I could tell. Everything OK?" she said, sensing that he wasn't totally there.

"Yeah, yeah. Was just thinking about something."

"Anything you wanna talk about?"

"Nope."

"Thought so."

They ordered some food and spent the next few minutes small talking, neither saying anything of much substance. Mia figured she'd wait a little while until she dropped the news on him as she was sure he wouldn't like what she had to tell him. She waited until they finished eating before she spat out what was on her mind. Part of her was nervous to talk to him about it, knowing he would vehemently disapprove of her actions.

"Have you heard anything about Susie's case lately?" she said, keeping her tone light deliberately, and running her fingers through her hair as a distraction.

Recker just shook his head. "No. Nothing new. Police still don't seem to have any leads to work from."

"They don't seem to be trying very hard."

"I know it's tough for you," Recker said.

"Yeah. That's why I started doing something about it on my own."

Recker squinted his eyes slightly, unsure what she meant, but not liking the sound of it. "What exactly have you done?"

"I started looking into some things."

"Such as?"

"Just going through her contacts, appointments, and clients to see if she had a relationship with anybody outside of work. Or maybe if any of them have a particularly violent past," Mia said, squirming uncomfortably on her seat in readiness for Recker's response.

Recker made a face and sighed, clearly unhappy. "Mia, we've already done that. When we were looking for her, we checked the backgrounds of all her clients. Only a couple had any type of criminal background and those that did, were home at the time she disappeared."

"I know. That's why I dug a little further."

"You what?"

She cleared her throat as she explained. Even when Recker didn't try to be, knowing his past history, he could be an intimidating figure. And she knew he didn't approve of anything she said or was about to say.

"I started digging into the backgrounds of some of the relatives of some of her clients," Mia stated.

"Mia."

"Don't Mia me. One of my best friends, someone I've known since college, someone I was roommates with, was killed and stuffed in a car," she said, on the verge of crying. "It's been three months since she was found and nobody, including you, seems to give a damn about what happened to her. The police don't seem to care, you give me the runaround, what else am I supposed to do?"

Knowing she was frustrated, Recker tried to be patient with her. "I know you're hurt and angry, but you can't do this."

"Why?"

"To be perfectly honest, you don't know what you're doing."

"Well someone has to do something. Nobody else is."

"Let the authorities handle it."

"We both know that if they haven't found who did it by now, the odds are only going to get worse as time moves on," Mia said.

"Maybe. But you're not equipped to do this."

"Well I've already started. I can't just go on living, knowing that Susie's killer is out there roaming the streets and no one seems to care."

"I told you that I would start looking into it as soon as I got some free time," Recker said, trying hard to stay patient.

"Which is never. Mike, you never have free time. It almost takes an act of God for you to just take a few minutes to have lunch with me," she replied in frustration.

Recker looked down at the table. The comment stung a little bit even though he knew she wasn't wrong and was well within her rights to feel that way. Mia read his face and saw that she'd hurt him a little with her words.

"I'm... I'm sorry. I didn't mean that," Mia said.

"Yes you did. It's OK. You're not wrong."

"I know you're busy and you have a lot on your plate. Not that you ever talk much about what's on it. But I know you're stretched thin already and I've already asked you more than I should about it. And I know it's not your job to look into my own personal things so I'm not even going to ask you anymore."

Recker took a few seconds to think of something to try and convince her to not pursue her intentions any further.

"What do you think's going to happen if you actually find something?" Recker asked.

"If I get close enough to actually start putting some pieces together, then I'll take what I've learned to the police."

"If you get that far."

"What's that supposed to mean?" Mia wondered.

"Because you're not a trained investigator. You're not experienced in this line of work. You make one wrong move, take one wrong step, and it could be last. If you start looking into things and ruffle the wrong feathers, you might be the next one that's stuffed in the trunk of a car," Recker warned.

"I'm willing to take that chance."

"I'm not willing to let you take that chance."

"Mike, you're not gonna stop me," she told him.

"I'm not gonna let you do this and possibly get yourself killed."

"Would it really matter to you?"

Recker leaned back, trying not to let her hurtful words get to him. He knew it was more frustration and emotion talking than anything.

"You know I care about you or else I wouldn't be here," Recker said.

"I know. I shouldn't have said it. I guess I'm not feeling myself today," she sorrowfully replied.

"I promise you that I will start looking into it."

"When?"

"As soon as I get some time."

Mia rolled her eyes and sighed, weary from hearing that line before. "I know you mean well, Mike, but I don't want to wait forever for you. I'm gonna keep looking into things on my own. If you get some free time tomorrow, or next week, or next month, then great. But I can't wait for you."

Recker also sighed, knowing there was nothing he could say that was going to change her mind. They sat there for a few more minutes, mostly in silence, both of them rather uncomfortable after their exchange. Eventually, Mia excused herself, saying she had to go home and get ready for work, having the night shift. Recker wasn't sure she was being truthful or whether she was about to do something that both of them would regret by investigating on her own. Recker didn't take his eyes off her as she walked out of the diner. He watched out the window as Mia got into her car and drove away.

Recker sat there for a little while longer, just thinking about the conversation they just had. He felt like he had let Mia down. He thought he should've done what he wanted to do in the first place and bring Hanley's killer to justice. If he had, then Mia wouldn't be in the obvious amount of pain that she was. Recker didn't blame her a bit for the way she was talking or feeling. He thought back to how he felt in the days after he learned that somebody had killed Carrie. Or the pain that he was still feeling. He didn't think that losing a friend, even a close one, was comparable to losing a wife or husband, a parent, a child, or even a brother or sister. But he knew the pain could still be severe. Severe enough for someone to do something that they shouldn't. Something such as seeking revenge or trying to investigate matters on their own when they were clearly out of their element.

He knew he couldn't let her do what she was planning, at least not alone. Recker was the only one who could help her, outside of the police, who seemed to have put the case on the back burner. He was going to go back to the office immediately to let Jones know that he had to get back on the case and insist that it wasn't up for debate. He knew the professor would likely try to talk him out of it once more, but Recker couldn't let that happen again. And while he was at it, he was going to have a much sterner conversation about the whereabouts and progress, or lack thereof, about Agent 17. Recker was through waiting and getting the runaround. There was something tugging at him that Jones had already found Agent 17 and was just holding off on telling him out of fear that Recker would leave immediately.

Once Recker got back to the office, Jones could

instantly tell that something was wrong. Recker had the face of someone who was about to blow his cool, a mad scowl seeming to be permanently attached. Recker walked up to the desk and stopped, not saying a word. He just stared at the professor.

"I was going to ask how your lunch was but by the look of your face I'd say it didn't go so well," Jones stated.

"We need to have a talk."

"Oh?" Jones asked, fearful of the subject they were about to embark on. "About?"

"Two different subjects," Recker answered.

"I take it one of them will involve Mia?"

"It does."

"OK, let's start with that then," Jones said. "What exactly is the problem with her?"

"She's hurting, and she's angry. It's been three months and nobody seems to give a damn that her friend was killed."

"We both know that's not the case."

"Isn't it?" Recker asked. "If you'd have let me done what I wanted to when I found her body, we wouldn't even be having this conversation right now."

"We both know that it was for the best that we left it alone."

"No, we don't know that. I don't. The police have put the case on the back burner. You told me yourself the last time you hacked into the police files the other day that they hadn't even updated the case files in a month," Recker said. "They've moved on."

"We had other cases... our own cases, to work on,"

Jones responded. "As I said, we're not in the revenge business."

"But we are in the helping business. And right now we need to help Mia."

"In what regards?"

"She's out there investigating on her own. She's starting to talk to people and look at things," Recker revealed, getting a sigh out of Jones who knew that was a bad idea.

"So what do you suggest?" Jones asked.

"We both know that she's not gonna let this go. And it might not be right away, maybe it'll take some time, but we both know she's intelligent, resourceful, stubborn, and persistent. Eventually, if she pursues this, and she will, she's gonna strike a nerve with someone. She'll talk to someone who knows something. And that someone will get jumpy. And that's going to put her in danger."

Though Jones empathized with Recker's position, he wasn't so sure the situation was as dire as his friend was predicting. After all, Mia wasn't a trained investigator. Jones wasn't sure she'd get far into her investigation at all.

"At the risk of sounding cold hearted and uncaring, what makes you so sure that she won't give up after a week, despondent that she's unable to turn up anything of consequence?" Jones wondered.

"Like I said, she's strong willed. She's angry, and she's hurting. That's not a good combination. Trust me, I've been there."

"Comparing the two of you is not quite the same thing. One of you is a trained assassin skilled in the art of this type of warfare and one of you is a nurse. That hardly compares."

"Maybe so. But I'm telling you, she will not let this go," Recker warned.

"I think you're being a bit presumptuous in how far she can take this and what kind of danger she uncovers. For all we know it was a completely random act of violence against Ms. Hanley, someone who she never met before that incident. Someone who could be in an entirely different state by now," Jones rebuffed.

"You don't really believe that, do you?"

"What?"

"That it was random," Recker answered.

"I really have no idea. And neither do you."

"I know it wasn't random. Whoever did it, was someone she knew."

"And how do you know that?"

"She was strangled, then shot, then stuffed in the trunk of her car. There's nothing random about that. That's at the hands of someone who's made it personal. That's someone who's angry," Recker told him. "A stranger wouldn't bother to go through the hassle of doing all those things."

"Perhaps you're right. But I don't think we can spare the time right now to look into the case. I know that's what you're suggesting," Jones replied.

"I'm not suggesting. I'm telling you. I'm back on the case."

Jones looked despondent, knowing that he was losing the argument. He knew that Recker would put Mia's interests ahead of any other cases they were working on at the moment and was worried that other people would get hurt in the meantime. Things that could have been prevented if they weren't sidetracked with personal entanglements.

"And to what end are you going to pursue this?" Jones asked.

"What do you mean?"

"Well, how long do you plan to work on this?"

"As long as it takes," Recker answered.

"And what happens if you find the person who did this? Just turn the information over to the police?"

"I'll finish the case my way."

"Which means what?"

"I'll put two bullets in their head," Recker bluntly replied. "Then it'll be over."

"That's not how we're supposed to operate."

"That's how I operate."

"And what of our other cases?" Jones wondered. "There are other people out there who need help as well."

"I can work more than one case at a time. I can help them while helping Mia at the same time."

"Would you be doing this if it was someone other than Mia?"

"Of course not," Recker responded.

"I thought so."

"Listen, she's a friend and I care about her. I'm not about to let her get mixed up in something that she's ill-equipped for and unprepared to handle. And no, it's not because I'm falling in love with her. I know that's floating around somewhere in that head of yours."

"Just making sure I know where you stand on things," Jones said.

"I would do the same thing for you if it was you in her shoes," Recker told him.

Jones knew that there was nothing he could do or say that would change Recker's mind. Though he still wasn't sure that Mia would find the danger that Recker expected her to find, Jones had never seen him so persistent on anything before. There was no talking him out of it. And he knew better than to keep trying and fighting a losing game. He did worry about what would happen if Recker did find the culprit of Hanley's murder. It was now personal to Recker, and Jones hoped that he wouldn't get careless and make a mistake that would somehow compromise the two of them or their operation.

"When exactly do you plan on starting this little side escapade of yours?" Jones asked.

"No time like the present," Recker replied.

"Very well then. I guess we need to get started then, don't we?"

2

After an hour of working to put together some information that they could go off to re-start the Hanley investigation, Recker still hadn't said anything about the lack of progress in regards to Agent 17. Though it was still eating at him, the fire inside had subsided slightly as he continued looking into the case of Mia's friend. Not that he was happy about letting it go, but he figured right now they needed all their energy focused on the other things they were working on.

Once again, he'd put it to the side for the betterment of others, even though it frustrated him. It seemed all he ever did was push it away so they could work on other things. Recker's hatred for the man who killed Carrie was still burning strong. It never waned even for a second. At some point, if he really wanted to atone for her death, he was going to have to be selfish and put his own wants and needs above those of others. Just one time.

Taking a break for a few seconds between the different cases he was juggling, Jones looked over at his friend and thought there was still something wrong. Recker looked like a man with some heavy baggage on his shoulder. From some of his facial expressions, Jones thought he looked frustrated for some reason. It appeared to him like Recker had more on his mind than he was letting on.

"So are you going to tell me about the second thing?" Jones finally asked, remembering Recker's words when he first got back to the office.

"The second thing?"

"You said we were going to talk about two different subjects but we only got around to talking about one of them."

"The other one can wait," Recker dejectedly replied.

"If you prefer... though I can tell something else is on your mind. Might be good to air it out so you can concentrate on this with a clear head."

Recker thought about it for a minute and decided Jones was right. It was time to let it out and not hold back like he had been doing.

"Fine. You wanna know what else is bothering me?" Recker said, sounding mad.

"I'm not so sure now," Jones teased, a little worried about his anger level.

"It's your commitment level."

"My commitment level?"

"Not for this. I mean that little software program of yours."

"Oh. I see."

"Are you actually even running anything? Is it even working? I mean, every time I've ever asked you about it, all you say is that it's close. Or it's not quite ready. I feel like all you're doing is feeding me a line of crap," Recker vented. "I don't think you're looking at all. Or if you are, not very hard. You never really wanted to pursue this or wanted me to pursue it. And I think you're doing everything you can to put it off and postpone it as long as possible. Well I'm tired of waiting."

"And you want an update," Jones surmised.

Recker just shook his head. "No, I don't want an update. Cause your updates are just giving me the runaround. I want to know where he is. Now."

Jones gulped and looked over at his computer, thinking carefully as to how he should respond. He knew this day would come at some point, with Recker questioning his efforts on the search. Jones just hoped the day wouldn't come for a while yet. After thinking about his different options, and the consequences of each, he thought it best to come clean with his highly dangerous partner.

"You are correct," Jones softly stated.

"About which part?"

"All of it. You're right. I've never been enthused about participating in this project. I haven't given it my best efforts, I've kept you in the dark, I've tried to stall, and for that I do apologize."

"I don't want apologies," Recker replied. "I just want you to find him. If you can't, or won't, then just say it so I can search on my own."

"No. I told you I would help you and I will."

Recker threw his hands up. "When? I don't wanna sit here and listen to you give me nonsense for another year."

"And you won't have to. I guess I've been fearful of what would happen when the day came that I could locate Agent 17 for you," Jones told him.

"I already told you what I'd do."

"Yes, I know. That's what's frightened me. In the time that we've been doing this, we've done such great things, incredibly important things. And I guess I worry that you're going to throw away all that we've accomplished in such a short time to pursue your own vendetta."

"You're right. We've accomplished a lot. And we're gonna keep on accomplishing a lot. Me finding Agent 17 is not going to change that," Recker said.

"I guess I'm not sure I believe that. Part of me has felt that once you found him, you would never come back. I know that finding him has always been your number one goal. I guess part of me was hoping, however foolish it may have been, that as time went on that you would put that part of your life behind you and focus more on this one."

"The love of my life was taken from me. There's nothing on this world or any other that would make me forget about that. And as long as he's out there, a part of me will never be totally here."

It was an emotional heart to heart talk the two men were having, one that was much needed and overdue. While they'd known each other, they avoided talking about their true feelings on the subject and danced around it as much as possible.

"And when you find him? What then?" Jones asked.

"I'll kill him. Just like I said."

"And after that?"

"I'll come back here and continue the work that we've been doing," Recker replied.

"You make it sound like it will be that easy."

"That's all there is to it. If you'd have found him when we first started this, I honestly don't know if I would've come back. But this has become like a home, at least as much as one as I've ever had. There's people I care about here. I give you my word that I will be back."

"And what if you can't come back? What if he kills you?"

"That's not gonna happen," Recker forcefully said.

"You make it sound like you're hunting someone who's blissfully unaware or some kind of pencil pusher," Jones told him. "Your adversary is someone who's just as capable as you are, just as skilled as you are, just as dangerous as you are, someone who knows the same tricks that you do. He could just as easily kill you."

"You know, if I'd found him before we started all this, before I met you, I probably wouldn't have even cared about the outcome. I wouldn't have cared if I came back. As long as he was dead... I wouldn't have cared if I joined him in the afterlife, if there is one, or buried in the ground, or whatever it is that people believe in."

"And that's the belief and attitude that concerns me," Jones said.

"But I'm not that guy now. Not with you, and Mia, and the work we've got going on here. But I still hear those words he said to me. Every day, I replay it in my mind, over and over again. Not one day since Carrie's been gone that I haven't thought about that night. Not one," Recker said, his eyes getting glossy. "I can never be truly free from what haunts me and tears me up inside until the day he's no longer breathing. I need him to see that it's me, that I'm the one that's ending his existence."

Jones could feel the pain that Recker bore. He wore it on his shoulders every day. And now that Recker was pouring his emotions out on his sleeve, Jones knew he didn't have the right to keep the secret he'd been hiding any longer. Whether he agreed with Recker's decision or not, he was clearly still hurting, and it wasn't up to Jones to prevent him from healing or seeking closure. No matter what the outcome, the decision wasn't his to make. It was Recker's. Jones would just have to hope for the best.

"I'm afraid I have something else to tell you," Jones said, his voice barely above a whisper. "I haven't been honest with you."

"I know. You already said that."

"No. There's more. I've been keeping a secret from you and since you have... expressed your feelings so deeply to me, I feel I need to share it."

"What is it?" Recker asked.

"I've already found him."

"What?" Recker asked in disbelief.

He was sure there was no way he heard what he thought he did. There was no way Jones was saying that he'd found Agent 17. Recker was positive he was going to say another name. Someone who was possibly connected to the man he was seeking all this time.

"I've already found him. Agent 17," Jones revealed.

"When?"

"About two weeks ago."

Shocked, Recker just stared at Jones, unable to form any words that would do the situation justice. He wasn't sure whether he should feel anger at being kept in the dark for the last two weeks, whether he should be furious at the professor for not being truthful, or whether he should be happy that the only thing he'd been living for all this time was finally within reach.

For his part, Jones felt like digging a hole and crawling into it. With Recker's incredulous reaction, the professor felt horribly for not coming forward with the information sooner. He wouldn't have blamed Recker if he got up off his chair and belted him across the face. With Recker's intimidating stare, Jones had trouble looking at him, knowing how disappointed in him Recker must've been. He felt ashamed of himself for not revealing the information as soon as he learned of it.

"I'm not going to apologize for my actions," Jones stated. "Not because I'm not sorry, but because I know those words aren't good enough or strong enough to satisfy you, as they shouldn't. I just hope that you will eventually forgive me for misleading you."

Recker finally broke his stare and leaned forward, rubbing his hands together. He let his eyes dance around the room, shifting between parts of the floor and wall, thinking about the best way to express himself. He didn't want to just emotionally blow up at Jones, unable to control himself, so he just let everything sink in for a minute until he could calmly rationalize everything.

"So were you ever gonna tell me?" Recker wondered. "I mean, were you just gonna sit on this forever?"

"I don't know." Jones shrugged. "I don't know. It's something that I wrestled with every day since his name finally popped up. There were times when I was close to saying something. But then there was another case, or another lead, or another situation that needed our attention, and I just let it slip away."

Though Recker was mad, and hurt, and felt betrayed, he was willing to put all that aside for the moment. If Jones had the information he needed, then Recker would deal with it at another time. Now wasn't the time to let his focus shift elsewhere. Now, finally, was the time to deal with Agent 17. And in the end, that was all that mattered.

"So where is he?" Recker asked.

"Right at this exact moment? I don't know," Jones answered.

Recker closed his eyes and took a deep breath, trying to control his anger. He surely could have become enraged if he so desired. But he was trying to keep his cool, only for the sake of finding his target.

"You had him. And you let him go," Recker whispered.

"Only for the moment," Jones reassured. "I can go back to where I located him and retrace his steps from that moment on. I can get a read on him again."

"How long will it take?"

"Give me a day or so and I should have it," Jones confidently stated.

"One day."

"One day. You have my word... for whatever that may be worth to you at the present time."

"Where'd you find him?" Recker wondered.

"Italy."

"What was he doing there? An assignment?"

"Yes. From what I can tell he'd been there approximately three days," Jones confirmed. "I got a hit on a report he submitted that his mission was completed."

"Where'd he go from there?"

"That I don't know. Like I said, I got sidetracked with another case we were working on and I lost his movements for the time being."

"So how do you know you're gonna be able to find him again?" Recker asked.

"Because now I know what I'm looking for," Jones answered. He reached into a desk drawer and pulled out a notepad with a bunch of names on it.

"What's this?" Recker wondered.

"Those are a list of some of his aliases. I wrote them down for the purpose of tracking him again."

"What makes you think he'll use one of them again?"

"Well, considering he's not on the run like you, I'm quite certain he'll be confident enough to use one of them rather quickly," Jones replied.

For the next couple of hours, Jones focused his attention only on finding Agent 17. With them being so close to knowing his whereabouts, spending a few more days on other matters would allow the mysterious agent to further slip through their fingers. The more they let time pass, the more Agent 17 could disguise his movements. As Jones typed away, Recker hovered over him, watching closely what he did. Though Jones understood Recker's eagerness at being so close to the man who killed his girlfriend, it still unnerved him a little bit.

"Why don't you go out for a while?" Jones asked, spinning around in his chair.

"Trying to get rid of me?"

"Not at all. It's just that it's a tad disrupting to feel you breathing on my neck."

Recker took a few steps back, getting the hint. "Just a little anxious I guess."

"I quite understand."

Recker then gave Jones some space. Instead of standing right behind him and watching him closely, Recker started pacing around the room. About every twenty minutes or so, he asked Jones the same question.

"How you making out?" Recker asked repeatedly.

"The same as the last time you asked," Jones replied. "It's coming along."

"You keep saying that."

"I understand your angst over the matter, Michael. But it's only been about five hours. I'm making progress."

"Can't you make it quicker?"

"You know as well as I do that tracing the movements of someone with multiple aliases, and who technically doesn't exist, in a government program that doesn't exist...

takes quite a bit of time," Jones answered. "I said it'd be about a day and it should still be that."

Recker sighed. "Fine."

"Go home, relax, see a movie, go out and about, do something. Come back tomorrow and I should have something for you."

Recker contemplated his options for a minute before finally agreeing. Although he was hesitant to leave, he figured it was better for his nerves if he did. He'd never before been so anxious to get someone's location, but then again, he never was on a mission before as personal to him as this one was. Part of him thought that if he left, something would go wrong, and they'd lose Agent 17's location for good. Recker then realized that his presence had no real bearing on whether they found the man or not since Jones was the one doing all the legwork.

"Fine. I'll go home and come back tomorrow," Recker said.

"Don't come early," Jones told him.

"Well what time would you like me to show up?"

"Early afternoon should suffice."

"You better have it by then."

3

Jones worked continuously throughout the rest of the day and night, hardly taking any breaks at all. He only slept for about four hours, knowing he was on a deadline that Recker would be strict about. He still felt badly about not telling Recker about finding Agent 17 a couple weeks before and was pressuring himself to re-find the man as quickly as possible. And that was before Recker's warning about it being ready. If he needed more time, he was sure Recker would understand, as long as it was a reasonable amount. Though he couldn't rule out bodily harm if he crossed the wrong side of Recker again. Jones was sure his friend would never do that to him, but there was a small piece of him that thought that Recker was so obsessed with finding Agent 17 that nothing was off the table with him.

Recker hadn't slept much either. Once he lay down, all he could think about was getting Agent 17 in his sights. He thought of almost every possible scenario in which their confrontation could go down. In every single one of them, the ending came with Agent 17 getting a bullet. Sometimes it was in the head, sometimes in the chest, but they all finished with Recker standing over the lifeless body of his victim.

Doing as Jones had requested, Recker spent the morning away from the office, giving the professor enough time to find their target. At least, Recker hoped he'd given Jones enough time. If Jones told him that it'd take more time, there was no telling how Recker might respond. However, he responded, it wasn't likely to be pretty. And it definitely wouldn't be calm. He wanted Agent 17's location, and he wanted it today. No more excuses.

Recker finally rolled into the office a little after two o'clock, and in his opinion, giving Jones plenty of time. Once Jones heard the door open, he looked at his partner arriving, then looked at the clock. Recker came a little later than Jones had anticipated. With how anxious Recker was, Jones envisioned him coming a minute after twelve. He figured that was Recker's definition of early afternoon.

Recker thought that he'd be able to tell by Jones' face how the search was going, without him having to say a word. But surprisingly to him, he couldn't get a read on it. Jones didn't look especially happy, indicating that he found their guy, but he didn't look stressed or worried either, indicating that he couldn't find him yet. Recker walked right up to the edge of the desk where Jones was sitting, ready to get a report.

"Well?" Recker asked.

Jones looked up at him from the computer and opened his mouth to say something, but just froze, trying to think of the best way of putting his thoughts. Since the professor didn't come right out with it, Recker assumed that he couldn't locate him.

"You didn't find him yet, did you?" Recker asked.

Jones put his index finger in the air as he replied. "I am almost there."

Recker sighed and threw his hands up in frustration. "I've heard that before."

"No, seriously, I am almost there," Jones replied, turning his attention back to the computer, resuming his typing.

"How much longer now?"

"An hour. Tops."

"One hour?" Recker asked, not convinced of the time frame.

"Guaranteed. He's back in the United States," Jones revealed. "I'm extremely close. I've tracked his last flight back here and I'm seeing where he went from there."

"What flight?"

"He landed in New York."

"New York?" Recker asked, surprised at how close they physically were.

"He's not still there though. That's what I'm currently tracking."

Not wanting to bug Jones too much and throw his

concentration off since he seemed to be so close, Recker resumed his position from the previous day, pacing throughout the room as he awaited word that their target had been found. Though he wanted to ask every few minutes how it was going, Recker refrained from doing so. Even though he didn't ask the question, he looked at Jones almost constantly, trying to read his face and actions as to whether he found him yet. After almost an hour exactly, Jones suddenly stopped typing, leaning back in his chair as he stared at the screen. Recker stopped his pacing as he anxiously awaited for Jones to say something.

"I've found him," Jones looked up and said.

Recker rushed around the desk and sat down next to Jones and looked at the screen with great anticipation. "Where is he?"

"Ohio. Just outside of Columbus to be exact."

"3248 Eddington Road," Recker read off the screen. "What is that?"

"It's a residential address," Jones answered. "It appears to be where he lives."

Recker quickly turned his head toward his partner at the revelation of having Agent 17's home address.

"I would temper your enthusiasm at having a quick and clean operation," Jones warned.

"Why's that?"

Jones switched screens and pulled up a picture of a woman holding a young child.

"Who are they?" Recker wondered.

"That would be his wife and two-year-old son."

Recker stared at the picture for a few moments.

"Does that change anything?" Jones asked. He thought that once Recker saw that the man had a young family, that maybe his thoughts on the operation might change. He clearly didn't know Recker as well as he thought.

"Changes nothing," Recker replied.

"If you kill him, you would tear this family apart," Jones reasoned. "A child will grow up without a father and a mother will lose her husband."

"Doesn't mean anything to me."

"How can you sit there and say that?"

"He killed an innocent person. And he did it happily. I'm not letting him off the hook for that just because he's married with a child," Recker answered. "He'll be lucky if I don't do to him what he did to me."

Taking a few seconds to think about his statement, Jones became horrified at the meaning, if he was correct in his assessment.

"Please tell me that doesn't mean what I fear it does," Jones stated.

Recker shrugged. "I dunno. You tell me."

"I hope that wasn't an indication that you would consider killing his wife and child."

Recker squinted his eyes like he was thinking, then shook his head. "I wouldn't kill a child."

Jones let out a sigh of relief. "Thank goodness for that. I would hope not. I thought I knew you better."

"The woman's another story," Recker said.

"Michael, I know you're consumed with rage at this man and I'm honestly not saying you're wrong in feeling that way. But you cannot kill innocent people just to satisfy your thirst for revenge," Jones pleaded. "She's an innocent woman who's probably blissfully unaware of her husband's dealings. You cannot let her take the fall for his perceived mistakes."

Recker leaned back and put his hand on his chin as he thought about it. Trying to think about it more calmly, he agreed with Jones' position. Regardless of his feelings for Agent 17, no matter how angry he was, no matter what he said or thought, he wouldn't knowingly kill an innocent person. As he was aware from his own time in the agency, he knew that the agent's wife most likely had no idea what was going on. No, he wasn't going to put anyone else's life in jeopardy. There was only one person who was going to pay the price and one person only.

"I won't take her out," Recker stated.

Jones closed his eyes and let out another sigh of relief. "Thank you for that."

"He's as good as dead though."

"I understand," Jones said.

"What's this guy's name, anyway?" Recker asked. "I'm getting tired of calling him Agent 17."

"Which one? He's got at least six names that I've identified," Jones told him.

"Whichever one he's going by right now."

"That would be Gerry Edwards."

Recker proceeded to read everything Jones had uncovered about Edwards. He read Edwards' files, reports, personal information, every assignment he'd been on, everything right down to the smallest details. He looked at several snapshots of Edwards, as well as his family.

According to the reports Recker was reading, Edwards seemed to be highly thought of within the agency. He was twenty-nine years old and had been in Centurion for about three years. He'd been married for six years to his college girlfriend and had a two-year-old son. On the surface, he seemed like a normal, regular guy. If somebody was reading his information, they wouldn't see anything that would give them pause about the type of person he was. Nothing specific seemed cold or callous. But they never heard what Recker did. As Recker looked at Edwards' picture, he heard his voice again, replaying their conversation in his mind once more. He thoroughly remembered how much pleasure Edwards got out of killing Carrie. There was no sorrow or sadness in his voice. There was no sense of regret about killing an innocent person. The longer Recker stared at the picture, the hatred and rage inside him grew as well. If he had a gun within reaching distance, he'd put a bullet right through the computer screen where Edwards' picture was.

Jones was reading some of the information as well, and periodically looked at Recker. As Recker silently sat there, staring at the screen, there was an intensity about him that worried Jones. He was concerned that in Recker's quest for revenge, or justice, that there was nothing that would stand in his way. Whether it be legal or illegal, moral or immoral. Jones worried that Recker would go to any lengths to get the man he was seeking. Not only did he worry about Recker crossing the line, Jones worried that he'd obliterate the line. Jones thought that underneath that silence, Recker's blood was boiling over. In an effort to calm him down, at least on the inside, Jones started talking to him to break his concentration on Edwards' picture.

"So I take it that you'll be leaving soon to take care of this matter," Jones stated.

"Yep."

"When do you plan on leaving?"

"I'll leave later tonight or in the morning," Recker answered.

"I thought so. What else do you need from me?"

"Just to help disguise my movements."

"What did you have in mind?"

"Well, after I kill him, the CIA's gonna wind up looking into it," Recker said. "They'll look into everyone coming in or out of town. That means I have to avoid cameras."

"That would leave out planes and trains for sure."

"That'd probably be their first inquiry. And if my face pops up..."

"Unless I were to hack into the camera system and temporarily disable it," Jones mentioned.

"No, too suspicious. Then they'll know the exact times someone boarded the planes and start narrowing the list down. Everything's gotta seem natural. Can't force anything or they'll know something's not right," Recker said.

"After that your best bet is either a bus or driving down yourself. Driving down there will take about fourteen hours or so."

"More than I'd like but I think it'll be the safest way to avoid detection."

"There are cameras on the freeways too," Jones noted.

"Yeah, but my vehicle won't come up on any lists and my license plate won't get a hit."

"What about the cameras at tolls?"

"If I put on a hat and wear it down low near my eyes, it won't pick my face up clearly."

"Well if you're planning on driving, you'd probably want to leave as soon as possible."

"I'll wait until the evening rush hour is over. No sense in fighting traffic along the way," Recker replied.

They spent another hour or so going over some plans. Recker figured if he left around six that he'd get to Columbus around eight if he drove nonstop. If he floored it, he could get there by six or seven in the morning. Hopefully, he could sit outside Edwards' house before he left and Recker could get him as he left in the morning.

"Could I make a suggestion?" Jones wondered.

"As long as it doesn't involve trying to talk me out of it."

"No, I know that would be an impossible task. If you decide on killing him..."

Recker just gave him a look. "I am killing him."

"Poor choice of words, whatever you decide to do, whenever you decide to do it, please don't do it in front of or inside his house."

"Why?" Recker asked.

"For the sake of his wife and child. Regardless of their relations, no wife should walk in and see her husband murdered in their own home. No child should see their father gunned down and bleeding to death inside their home. That should be his sanctuary from the world he's about to grow up in," Jones explained.

Recker frowned, letting Jones' reasoning rattle around inside his head for a few moments. Then he nodded, agreeing to his plea.

"OK. I'll make sure they don't see it," Recker told him.

"Thank you."

"You sure do have a lot of conditions, and a lot of empathy, for these people."

"Only for the innocent, Michael, only for the innocent. That is the business we're now in, remember? Protecting the innocent."

"Yeah."

"I fully understand your reasoning for killing Edwards. I completely accept what you're about to do and have no qualms about your actions. But I will fight for the lives of those who are not connected to his dealings," Jones said. "And what do you plan to do about Mia?"

"What do you mean? What about her?"

"You did suggest that we help her with her situation."

"She shouldn't run into any problems in the time that I'm gone," Recker responded. "I won't be gone that long."

"Do you think it might be wise if you told her that you were going to look into her situation so she backs off for the time being?" Jones wondered.

"Yeah, might be a good idea at that."

Recker tried calling Mia's cell phone a few times but couldn't get through, only getting her voicemail. Though he initially thought that she wasn't being honest that she had to work, he started to think maybe she was.

"Guess she had to work after all," Recker stated.

"I wouldn't be too sure about that," Jones replied.

"Why?"

"I've uh... gotten into the hospital time clock software program that they use."

"And?"

"And she hasn't clocked in yet," Jones answered.

"Then why wouldn't she be answering me?"

Jones simply shrugged. "Maybe she's already underway in her investigation. Didn't you say she said she already started?"

"Yeah, but I didn't think she really meant anything by it. I thought it was just her way of drawing me in," Recker responded.

"It would seem you misread her."

Recker sighed, not needing any problems to pop up right now. "Ah boy."

"What do you plan to do now?" Jones asked.

"Keep calling until she picks up."

Recker did as he said he would and kept calling Mia's phone every ten minutes. After an hour of unsuccessfully trying to get a hold of her, Recker was starting to get worried. He hadn't left any messages up to that point as he tried to avoid doing that, just in case the CIA could pick up his voice through one of their voice detection programs they sometimes utilized.

"Are you sure she's not at work?" Recker asked.

"Not unless she's working for free today," Jones

answered. "You could always try calling the hospital just to be sure."

"Yeah. Maybe I'll do that."

Recker then called the hospital and after a brief hold, was told that Mia wasn't scheduled to be in that day. After hanging up, he looked over at Jones and shook his head.

"She couldn't have gotten herself into any trouble already, could she?" Recker asked.

"Is that a question you want answered or are you just talking to yourself?"

"Both. I mean, what are the odds that she would've found something already that would make her not pick up the phone?"

Recker went back to repeatedly calling Mia's phone, calling it every five minutes again. Though he still wanted to avoid leaving messages, he finally relented and simply told her it was important and to call him back as soon as possible. He started pacing around the room again, his mind wandering about where she could have been. Another twenty minutes went by with still not a peep from Mia.

"Why don't you sit down?" Jones asked. "Pacing around the room isn't going to get her to call faster."

"I can't sit down."

"Can't you track her or something?"

"Possibly," Jones replied. "It'll take some time though."

Recker suddenly stopped and sat down. He put his head in his hands as he started to worry about what Mia might have gotten herself into already.

"What if she hasn't checked in by the time you want to leave?" Jones wondered.

"I'm not leaving until I know she's OK."

"You sound like a worried boyfriend."

In most circumstances, Recker might've taken offense to his implication of enhanced feelings for her. But in their current situation, he didn't pay much mind to it. He didn't even bother to reply. He looked at his phone again, thinking about calling her number one more time.

"I can't just sit here anymore," Recker stated.

"What do you plan to do?"

"I dunno. Go out and do what I do I guess."

"Where are you going to start?"

"Her apartment I guess. I'll figure out where to go from there."

"Maybe we could get Mr. Gibson involved?" Jones asked.

"Let me search her apartment first and see if I turn up anything."

Recker got up and walked over to the gun cabinet and started looking at which weapons he wanted to take with him. As soon as he picked up one of his handguns, his phone started ringing. Hoping that it was Mia, Recker rushed over to the desk to answer it. Jones, worried himself, leaned over and looked at the screen.

"It's Mia!" Jones shouted.

Recker reached across the desk to pick up the phone. "Where have you been?"

"Who taught you how to answer a phone?" she wondered.

"Are you OK?"

"Yeah, I'm fine. Why wouldn't I be?"

"Because I've been calling you for like two hours."

"Wow. You almost sound worried," Mia told him.

"I am worried."

"I didn't know you cared so much."

"Stop. You know I do," Recker said.

"I know. I'm sorry."

"Are you OK?"

"Yeah. I already said that."

"Then why haven't you been answering my calls?" Recker asked.

"I told you at the diner. I had to go to work. I'm just on my break now and saw you called."

"Mia?"

"Yeah?"

"I've already called the hospital, and they told me you weren't there and you weren't scheduled to work today," Recker revealed.

"Oh," she replied, knowing she was busted.

"Why don't you tell me where you really are?"

"I've been different places."

"So why did you tell me you had to work today when you didn't?" he asked.

"Because you wouldn't have liked it if I told you what I was really doing."

"Which was?"

"I told you I already started my own investigation into Susie's death," Mia explained.

Recker closed his eyes and sighed, afraid that was the answer he was going to get.

"I can hear you yelling under your breath," she told him.

"I'm not yelling."

"Not out loud at least."

"Mia, I'm just worried that you're gonna stumble into something that you're not prepared for," Recker said.

"I know. But I said that I wasn't waiting for anybody else anymore."

"Will you just do me a favor and step aside for a couple of days?"

"I'm not waiting anymore."

"Just for two or three days and then I promise you that I will help," he offered.

"You will? Why?"

"Because I know it's important to you and I'm worried that if I don't, then you'll get into something that you don't know how to get out of."

"What about your other cases?" Mia asked.

"I can still work my other stuff while looking into Susan's death. OK?"

"Yeah, but I've already talked to a couple people and I have some promising leads."

"Mia, please just wait a couple of days for me."

"Why do I have to wait? If you're interested in helping then why can't you get started right away?" she wondered.

"Because I have to go away for a couple of days," Recker told her.

"What? Why?"

"There's some old business that I have to finish up."

"Where are you going?" Mia asked.

"I can't really say."

"Of course you can't."

"It involves that night I told you about. When my old job tried to eliminate me."

"Oh. They found you?" she worried.

"No. But I found someone else. And it's something that I need to take care of right away."

"You are coming back, aren't you?"

"Of course I'm coming back."

"When are you leaving?"

"Tonight."

"Oh. So soon."

"Yeah. And I will be back in two or three days. Promise me you won't get into anything while I'm gone?"

"I mean, what if you don't come back?" Mia asked.

"I will be back. And when I am, I will do everything in my power to find Susan's killer. Promise me you'll wait till then?"

Mia paused, thinking of a response. "I promise I won't initiate anything."

"I guess that's as good as I'm gonna get from you," Recker replied.

"Probably."

4

Recker left Philadelphia just after seven and had been on the road for a little over five hours. For most of the drive, his mind was split between thoughts of revenge on Edwards and concern over Mia. Every time he tried to concentrate on how he'd kill Edwards, his mind would suddenly shift over to Mia's predicament. He only planned to be gone a day or two at the most, depending on how quick and easy he could get to Edwards. He assumed that Mia couldn't get into any real trouble in such a short amount of time since she just started her investigation. But then it occurred to him... what if she was further along than she let him know? Perhaps she started weeks earlier than she told him. She was already keeping it a secret from him so he wouldn't have put it past her if she started sooner than she initially told him. Recker was growing more worried that she'd get into something without him there to protect her. Figuring that Jones was still up, he called him to ask a favor.

"Hey. You weren't sleeping yet, were you?" Recker asked.

"No. I still had some things I was looking into."

"Still at the office?"

"Yes, why?"

"Just wondering."

"How are you making out so far?" Jones asked.

"Good. Should get there on time."

"Since I'm sure you didn't call to wish me pleasant dreams, what can I do for you?"

"Well aren't you cynical? Can't someone just call a friend to say hi without a reason?" Recker asked.

"Yes. But you've never done that before."

"Oh. Well, anyway, I was just calling to see if you can keep an eye on Mia while I'm gone."

"What do you mean, keep an eye on her?" Jones wondered.

"Just make sure she's not getting herself into any trouble."

"Should I follow her the entire day?"

"No. Just periodically call her. Make sure she's all right. Kind of hint at what she's doing."

"I guess I could do that. But if all you want me to do is call, then I don't see why you couldn't do that."

"Yeah, I don't think I'm high on her friend list right now," Recker said. "You're probably just as likely to draw any information out of her as I am, if not more."

"I suppose I could do that."

Jones continued working on some of the cases they'd start working on once Recker returned, assuming that he did return. There was still a part of Jones that feared that Recker wouldn't survive his encounter with Gerry Edwards. Even if Recker was successful in eliminating his target, there was always a possibility that he would get killed in his escape from the area. Jones buttoned everything up a little after two, knowing he'd have one more thing on his plate when he woke up with having to look after Mia.

Recker was right to be concerned about Mia's safety. His fears would turn out to be true as she hadn't been honest with him in regards to how far along she was with her investigation. The assumption was that she'd just started within the previous couple of days, when in reality, she was now in her fourth week. It started when she was helping Hanley's mother clean out her apartment. She found a piece of paper with a man's name and phone number placed inside a book that Susan had been reading. Joe Simmons was the name, and Mia had never heard her mention him before. Mia had gotten a hold of Hanley's appointment book and noticed that the name wasn't on it. She called the number listed on the paper but it was no longer in service. She wrestled on whether she should've handed the information over to either the police or Recker, but she figured both of them would just push her aside. Since neither of them seemed like finding Hanley's killer was high on their priority list, she was the only one who'd keep pressing to find the culprit.

It was after nine o'clock and Mia had just finished

eating breakfast when she sat down to look at some of her notes. After every person she talked to, she wrote down anything of note that they might have mentioned. She checked off every single person that was listed in Hanley's appointment book and mentioned to all of them whether they knew the name of the person that she found inside that book of Susan's. Nobody indicated that they knew who Simmons was. Her phone started ringing and when she looked at the ID screen, didn't recognize the number calling.

"Hello?" she greeted.

"I hear you're looking for someone," the voice said.

"Who is this?"

"I know where you can find Joe Simmons."

"Where?" Mia excitedly asked.

"Haddix Apartments on 5th street. Second floor, room 217. Go there at twelve and I'll give you everything I have on him."

"Who are you?"

"Doesn't matter."

"Who is this Joe Simmons? How did he know Susan?" Mia wondered. "Hello? Hello?"

There was no answer. Whoever was on the other end of the phone had already hung up. Mia sat there for another hour poring over her notes, trying to piece things together the best she could. Though she was a little hesitant at meeting someone who she didn't even know the name of, she was running out of leads to run down. If Recker was still there, she might've asked him to go with her, but since he wasn't, she'd have to go it alone. As she was reading her notes, her phone rang again. She quickly jumped at the phone thinking it might've been the same guy again, but this time she recognized the number.

"Mia, how are you?" Jones asked.

"Fine. You?"

"Good."

"Mike asked you to check up on me, didn't he?" Mia asked.

"Uhh..."

"It's OK. You don't have to lie or cover for him. I know he did."

"You're right. He did," Jones replied.

"I knew it."

"So is everything alright?"

"Everything's fine. You guys are such worrywarts," Mia told him.

"Well, with good reason. You're doing something you don't have much experience in. It's more difficult that it appears on the outside."

"I've been making out OK."

"So how much progress have you made so far? Perhaps I can start running things down here on my end?"

"I don't think I need any help with anything. I've already talked to everyone on her contact list and all her clients. Even friends and family of clients," she said.

Jones tilted his head, thinking it was strange that she was so far along already. "How can you have done all that already?"

"Huh?" Mia said, worried that she said too much.

"I find it peculiar that you could have accomplished so

much in such a short amount of time."

"Well, I haven't been sleeping much and I've been working around the clock."

"Considering you have a normal job, I don't see how it's possible you could have spoken to every one of her contacts so soon. Unless you've been at this much longer than we've suspected."

"No, just a couple days," Mia said.

"I may not be as adept at reading people as Michael is, but I do usually get a good impression as to when people are lying to me," Jones told her.

"Oh. Umm, I think I have someone on the other line."

"Mia?"

"Yes?"

"How long have you actually been working on this?"

"Uh... about four weeks."

"Oh dear," Jones stated.

"Everything's fine. There's nothing to worry about. Everything's fine," she reassured.

"And may I ask what you may be working on today?"

Mia wasn't sure she should tell him about the call she just received. He'd probably tell her it wasn't a good idea to go if she did. Apparently though, as Jones could attest, she wasn't a good liar. She figured she'd just kind of give a generic response without really answering the question.

"Uh... nothing," Mia told him.

"Nothing? Really?"

"I told Mike that I wouldn't initiate anything and I'm not."

Once again, Jones didn't feel like she was being truthful. "I get the sense that you're trying very hard not to tell me something."

"I don't know what you mean."

"So what do you have on your itinerary today?" Jones asked.

"Umm... nothing."

"You do realize I can check your phone logs if I have to, right?"

Mia didn't answer him and put her head down, slapping her hand against her forehead. She knew he was going to find out what she was up to whether she told him or not.

"Fine. I'm meeting someone at twelve who has some information for me," she finally relented.

"Mia... you told Mike..."

"I said I wouldn't initiate anything and I haven't. This person called me a little while ago and told me they knew something and wanted to meet. I'm just responding... not initiating."

"Semantics, Ms. Hendricks."

"Maybe."

"Who is this person that called?"

"I don't know. They didn't say."

"And you think this is wise to meet someone that you don't know who it is?" Jones asked.

"I don't know. I need answers and I'm willing to go wherever the leads take me."

"I'm not sure Michael would approve."

"Well he's not here, is he?"

"How do you know you're not walking into a trap or

something? How do you know this person really has information and isn't after something else? Or maybe they just want to harm you."

"I'm sure it'll be OK," Mia replied.

"I get the feeling that nothing I can say is going to dissuade you from going."

"That's right."

"You're as stubborn as Michael."

"Everything will be fine."

"Maybe. Perhaps I should go with you," Jones offered.

"No, that's really not necessary."

"At least give me the number of the person that called you so I can look into it."

Mia hesitated, not sure that she wanted the help at the moment. While she didn't initially think anything was suspicious about the phone call from the stranger, the more she thought about what Jones said, the more doubt started creeping into her mind. After another plea from Jones requesting the number, Mia agreed and gave it to him. They kept talking as Jones punched the phone number into his system. Just as he feared, the number didn't match up to anyone.

"Did you get anything?" Mia wondered.

"As I suspected, there's no match."

"How can that be?"

"It's most likely a prepaid phone," Jones replied.

"That doesn't mean something's up or I'm in danger or anything."

"No, but just the same, I do wish you'd reconsider going. At least until Michael returns."

"I'm not waiting," she defiantly said.

"Very well. Then I will insist on accompanying you."

"I don't think you really need to."

"It would put my mind at ease," Jones told her. "If I know you're going to this rendezvous and then I don't hear from you for a while, then my mind will wander with all sorts of terrible thoughts."

"Gee, thanks for the scare."

"Plus, Michael will never let me hear the end of it if he knows that I know that you're going to this thing and I didn't either stop you or go with you."

"So what you're really worried about is Mike giving you crap," Mia said.

"No. I care about you too."

"So have you heard from Mike since he left?" she asked. "How's his trip to Baltimore going?"

"Nice try but he did not tell you where he was going. And I can definitely say that it wasn't Baltimore," Jones answered.

"So you do know where he went."

"Yes, but I'm not at liberty to divulge that information."

"Of course you're not."

"But if you're curious as to his whereabouts, I can tell you that he's gotten there safely," Jones said.

"Is he done with whatever he was doing?"

"Not yet. He just text me a few minutes ago saying he arrived. He's not yet concluded his business."

"Why do you two always talk so cryptically?" Mia asked.

"It's for your own protection."

"That's what he says."

Mia agreed to let Jones go with him when she met the man that called her and agreed to meet at the Haddix Apartment complex. Both agreed to wait before going in until the other one arrived. Jones thought about letting Recker know what was going on but decided against it. He figured the less Recker had to worry about back in Philadelphia, the better his chances were for a successful outcome in Columbus. He didn't want Recker's mind cloudy or worried about anything other than completing what he felt he needed to do and getting back safely. If there was any trouble that arose from Mia's problem, Jones assumed he could take care of it for the time being.

Recker had just gotten to the Edwards address, a two story brick building a few miles outside of Columbus, Ohio. It was in a nice little community setting in a development with about three hundred other houses of similar stature. Recker estimated the worth of the houses to be in the four to five hundred thousand dollar range. Recker parked just up the street, still getting a good view of the Edwards house, but parking far enough away so as he wouldn't draw suspicion and be recognized. Edwards had a BMW X5 luxury crossover SUV registered to him but it wasn't parked in the driveway. There was a white Cadillac sedan still in the driveway, but that belonged to Tonya Edwards.

It was the scenario that Recker was dreading. Having to wait. With Edwards already gone, there was no telling when he might return. Recker was hoping to get to the house early enough that he could follow Edwards when he left in the morning. Now, he might have to wait all day which would delay his return to Philadelphia. It wasn't what Recker was hoping for. He hoped that he'd get there just before Edwards left and he could tail him, then kill him somewhere away from his home, then return to Philadelphia. But he realized that was the best-case scenario, not necessarily the most likely one.

As the time approached noon, Recker still hadn't observed any activity in or around the Edwards house. He figured Tonya Edwards either left with her husband or was having a quiet day at home with her son. According to their information, she didn't have a job and was a stay at home mother. Recker tried to stay busy by reading the files he printed out on Edwards. Though it wasn't complete, Jones had managed to dig up enough information about Edwards' time in the CIA, including several of his Centurion operations. Most of it seemed to be smaller assignments as the bigger missions usually were off the books or were only acknowledged by a small team of people. There was nothing in his files or reports about Recker's time in London or about Edwards killing Carrie in Florida. Not that Recker expected it to be there since those types of missions usually weren't noted anywhere except in the personal files of superiors. The CIA usually didn't chance that type of information being written anywhere within agency files for fear of leaks or hacks. Those reports were usually only handled in the files of the CIA Director or whoever was in charge of the Centurion project.

Assuming he had some time to kill, Recker started wondering what was going on back in Philly. He had sent Jones a few texts within the past half hour but didn't get a reply to any of them. Recker thought it was a little strange as Jones usually responded quickly to texts and phone calls. The professor was usually in the office and near his phone so Recker couldn't think of any reason why he would be ignoring his texts. The only thing he could think of is if something important had come up and Jones was in the field for some odd reason. Seeking to put his mind at ease, Recker tried calling Jones several times, still not getting an answer.

"Not this again," Recker whispered, not wanting to go through the same thing that he did with Mia the day before.

Recker tried calling a couple more times, each time getting a little more frustrated with each call that went unanswered. Finally, after about fifteen minutes of struggling to get through, Jones finally picked up.

"What took so long?" Recker wondered.

"I'm sorry. I just had other things I was attending to," Jones responded. "Is everything all right there?"

"Yeah. Edwards wasn't here when I arrived. Looks like I gotta wait it out for a while."

"Oh. So why are you calling then?"

"Just making sure everything's OK there," Recker answered. He thought he detected the sounds of cars and a horn in the background, making him wonder where Jones was going. "Are you driving somewhere?"

"How could you know that?" Jones asked.

"It's kind of what I do for a living."

"Indeed."

"Where are you going?"

"I'm just checking on something."

"You're a lousy liar, David. What is it that you don't want to tell me?" Recker asked.

"Well without you here, I have to go out into the field for a little bit."

Recker wasn't going to just accept that for an answer. Before leaving, they agreed to not pursue any of their upcoming cases until Recker returned. He looked at each one of the cases and remembered the names of the parties involved.

"I thought you agreed to wait till I got back?" Recker asked.

"Well, something came up that I need to check into. Shouldn't take too long."

"What case is it?"

"The uh... the Joe Simmons case," Jones said, wincing as he said it, hoping that Recker wouldn't pick up on the name.

It was a bad assumption as Recker knew the name wasn't familiar. Recker took the phone away from his ear and looked at it strangely as if he misheard the name. He knew the name wasn't among any of the cases they were beginning to look into. Even if it was a name dug up in the background, Recker didn't figure it'd be important enough for Jones to head out into the field already.

"Joe Simmons?" Recker asked. "Who's that?"

"You know, one of the cases I started working on."

"David?"

"Yes?" Jones dejectedly replied, knowing the gig was up.

"There was no Joe Simmons listed in any of the files. I checked them all before I left. So you're either making the name up to disguise something or it's something completely unrelated to any of our cases. Which is it?"

"Just let it go for now. I'll explain everything to you when you return," Jones answered.

"You really want to go this route?"

"I don't want your focus to be taken off what you're currently doing. I'll handle things here."

"There's nothing wrong with my focus. What's going on?"

"I don't want any distractions for you," Jones repeated.

"David, something's going on and I want you to tell me the truth right now," Recker tersely replied.

"Well..."

Recker didn't even let him finish, thinking he had it figured out. "It's Mia, isn't it?"

"Well..."

"Haven't even been gone one full day," Recker said to himself. "What's the problem?"

"Well, first problem is your initial estimate on how far along she was with her investigation," Jones told him.

"She didn't just start a few days ago?"

"Try four weeks."

Recker closed his eyes for a moment and sighed, afraid to hear what she'd gotten herself into. He rubbed his forehead as he waited for an explanation. "She promised she wouldn't do anything until I got back."

"Well, as she told me, she only promised not to initiate anything. Unfortunately, she didn't promise she wouldn't respond to something."

"What happened?"

"She received an anonymous phone call to meet someone at an apartment complex to give her information on Joe Simmons," Jones explained.

"Who is this Simmons?"

"Apparently Mia found the name stuffed inside a book in Hanley's apartment when she was helping Susan's mother clean the place out."

"So she's meeting this person?"

"That would be correct."

"And I take it you're going with her?" Recker asked.

"Correct again."

"Well, thank you for that."

"I just hope we're not walking into something we're not equipped for," Jones said.

"Why do you think that?"

"I traced the number that called Mia and it came back to a prepaid phone."

"What time's the meeting?"

"In about ten minutes," Jones answered.

"I hope you're packing some iron with you."

"Though I sincerely hope it doesn't come to that, yes, yes I am."

5

Jones agreed to keep Recker updated with whatever information they learned from this anonymous meeting. Recker wasn't comfortable that they were even going to begin with, but being so far away, there was nothing he could do about it. Knowing that the two closest people he had left in his life were going to what sounded like a dangerous meeting, Recker was extremely anxious to get a call or text from Jones when it was over. Jones was right about Recker being distracted once he learned what was going on. Recker would continue staring at the Edwards house for the next half hour but his mind wasn't really there. Instead, his thoughts were turning to the situation that was five hundred miles away. He kept his phone clenched tightly in his hand as he waited for his ringer to go off. Until he got that call, his concerns over their safety was what was first on his mind.

Jones had gotten to the Haddix Apartments a few

minutes before Mia did. He waited in front of the building for her until she arrived. Mia quickly peeled into the parking lot and rushed to the building where Jones was waiting. The Haddix Apartments had seen better days. It was in dire need of a facelift. Though it wasn't a slum of a building, most of the residents were in the lower income group, and quite a few were on the other side of the law. The two of them just stood there looking at the building for a minute, neither sure what they were stepping into.

"Not exactly Rittenhouse Square or Society Hill, is it?" Jones asked.

"Not exactly."

"So what do you want to do?" Jones asked, hoping she'd forget the whole thing and turn around and walk back to her car.

Mia pulled out her phone to check the time. It just turned twelve. "Well, I guess we better get up there. If we're too late, I don't know if whoever it is will wait too long."

"Maybe that's not such a bad thing."

"You don't have to come up with me if you don't want to," Mia told him.

"I'm going wherever you're going."

Even though it was still against his better judgment, Jones put his arm out to indicate he was following her lead. They walked through the front doors and saw a sketchy looking character sitting on the floor and smoking a joint. They immediately noticed the elevator right in front of them and also stairs down the hallway to both sides of them.

"Stairs or elevator?" Mia asked.

"Elevator," Jones replied. "Who knows what we might see if we take the stairs."

They stepped inside the elevator, and Mia hit the button for the second floor. They each had an uneasy feeling in their stomachs, though neither of them contemplated turning back at that point. Mia figured it was more to do with her nerves, not having to do much of this sort of work before, rather than thinking they were in any kind of danger. Jones on the other hand, was more nervous because he was afraid that they were walking into something that they weren't prepared for. And although he used to be part of the NSA, and now worked with Recker, he still wasn't used to being out in the field in these situations. His value was behind the scenes and behind a computer. Field work wasn't exactly his forte. But, with Recker absent, he really didn't have a choice.

Once the elevator doors opened, the pair stepped out into the hallway. They stood there for a moment just looking at their surroundings. They didn't see anything out of the ordinary and began walking, looking at the numbers on the doors as they passed. At the end of the hall was room 217. As they approached, they could see that the door was slightly ajar. They could see that a light was on inside and put their ear up to the door though they couldn't hear any noise. They stood there silently and motionless for a minute, waiting to hear something that would indicate somebody was in there. But there was nothing. Mia just looked at Jones and took a deep breath, ready to continue. She quietly knocked on the door, barely loud enough for even Jones to hear, let alone anyone inside. Jones stepped in front of her and pushed the door open a little farther, big enough for him to get his head through and peak inside.

"Hello? Anyone here?" Jones asked.

They didn't get a reply and Jones pushed the door open all the way, taking a quick look around the room. He looked back at Mia and nodded for her to follow him inside. As they moved throughout the room, noticing their surroundings, there wasn't much to the apartment. There was a small, beat up looking couch with a few holes in it that appeared to be at least ten or twelve years old. Right in front of that was a small card table that looked more like something for a child. Jones checked the bedroom and found a futon folded out into a bed alongside a night table with a lamp sitting on it. Mia went to the kitchen and checked the cabinets and refrigerator. If someone was living there, they didn't have a big appetite. There were only a couple of items in the refrigerator and the only thing in the cabinets were some paper plates and plastic cups. After looking in their respective rooms, Mia and Jones met back up in the living room.

"Do you think someone's even living here?" Mia asked.

"I checked the address before we left and there is a Joe Simmons that is renting the place," Jones answered.

"So was it him that called me and asked to come here? Or was it someone else who knew that he lived here?"

"I guess that's the question that needs answering. But I think we should be leaving."

"Leaving? Already? We just got here," Mia objected.

"Yes, but if the person that called you was not Joe Simmons, and he walks through that door and sees two people standing here in his apartment, I don't think I have to tell you what might happen after that," Jones told her.

"But what if it was him?"

"Then he'll call you again," Jones said, grabbing her arm.

Mia shook her arm free of Jones' grasp, wanting to stay a little longer. "No, I want to get to the bottom of this."

"Mia, we don't know exactly what we've walked into here. I think it best if we leave now."

"Well, why was the door already open?" she asked.

"I have no idea. Perhaps he forgot to close it or maybe he just stepped outside for a minute thinking he'd be back shortly. In any case, I don't think it wise for us to remain here and surprise whoever it is that returns," Jones pleaded.

"But what if this person knows what happened to Susie?"

"What if this person *is* what happened to Susan?"

Mia was starting to come around to Jones' way of thinking and figured if this person did have information for her, then he would've been there. Jones offered to do some more research on Simmons if Mia agreed to leave right then and there. The hair on the back of Jones' neck was standing up as he wasn't getting a good feeling upon being there. Something seemed wrong to him. Though Jones did a precursory check on the address of the apartment, due to time constraints, that was about as far as he got into the man's background. Since Mia's meeting was so soon, he didn't have time to further explore Simmons's history or if he had a criminal past.

"So you'll let me see where you and Mike work your magic?" Mia asked.

"No. But I promise I'll get on it right away."

"You're not gonna cut me out, are you?"

"We'll discuss it in detail once we get out of here," Jones hurriedly replied, trying to rush Mia along so they could get out of there before someone else showed up.

Jones started walking to the door, with Mia right behind him, and removed his phone from his pocket to give Recker a call and let him know what was going on. Just as they got to the frame of the door, a man jumped out from the side and struck Jones in the head with a gun. Jones instantly fell to the ground as his phone flew out of his hand across the hall. He lost consciousness and began bleeding from the top of his head.

"David!" Mia yelled, kneeling down to check on Jones' condition.

She looked up at the professor's attacker, who was simply standing there and staring down at them. He was a younger guy, mid-twenties, blonde hair, athletic build. He had a slight smile on his face, seemingly impressed by his work in striking down one of his visitors. Mia tried tending to Jones' head the best she could, though his attacker started to move her along.

"Get in," he told her, waving his gun in the direction of the apartment.

Mia slowly got up, fearful of what the man was then going to do. She retreated back into the apartment, never taking her eyes off the gun-toting stranger. With Jones still knocked out, the man grabbed the back of the professor's shirt and dragged him back inside, closing the door behind them with his leg.

"Take out your phone and throw it down on the ground," the man said.

Mia complied with the request and tossed it on the floor near the man's feet. He reached down and took the handle of his gun to smash the screen to pieces.

"You got a gun on you?" the man asked.

"No."

"Turn around."

Mia turned around and faced toward the window as the man came up behind her and started patting her down to make sure she didn't have a weapon on her. He took a couple extra liberties in squeezing and grabbing her private parts.

"All right, turn around," the man told her.

"Who are you and what do you want?" Mia nervously asked.

"Don't you know? I'm Joe Simmons."

"You're the one who called me this morning."

Simmons just smiled and nodded. "Yeah. That was me."

"Why? What do you want? Why are you doing this?"

"You're getting too close."

Mia had a feeling she knew what he meant. "You killed Susie. Didn't you?"

"A rather unfortunate event," Simmons answered.

"Why?" Mia asked. She felt like asking a million other

questions but that was the only one that she could get through her lips.

"We had a date. Things started to get heated and then for some reason she started resisting. It got a little out of hand after that."

"A little out of hand? You killed her," Mia emotionally said.

"She shouldn't have slapped me like she did. Made me mad," Simmons unapologetically replied.

"You don't seem like it even bothers you in the least."

"Not the first time I've had to do something like that."

"How'd she even meet you anyway?" Mia wondered.

"My cousin was the parent of one of her patients. One day he asked if I could take the kid to see her cause he couldn't get off work. So after it was over I asked if I could take her out sometime," Simmons revealed.

"How many times did you go out with her?"

"Before I killed her? Just once. We had one date before the unfortunate mistake on her part."

Just listening to the man explain himself and keep referring to Hanley's death as an unfortunate event made Mia's blood boil. She'd never hated anyone as much as she did right at that moment. Unfortunately, there was nothing she could do about it. She wasn't armed and wasn't sure how she was going to get out of the situation.

"So how'd you find out about me?" Simmons asked. "Nobody else knew about me. Nobody else was aware we knew each other. Not even the cops. What tipped you off?"

"When I was cleaning out Susie's apartment I saw a

piece of paper in one of her books. It had your name on it."

Simmons let out a slight laugh. "I knew it had to be something stupid like that. You talked to my cousin last week and when you mentioned my name, he called me to let me know. I've been keeping tabs on you for the last week."

"So what are you going to do with us?" Mia wondered, hoping not to hear what she thought she would.

Simmons shrugged, waving his gun around. "Well, unfortunately for you, you now know my secret. You know who I am, you know what happened to your friend, and I just can't let you go walking around with that kind of knowledge, now can I?"

"And if I say that I won't tell anyone?"

Simmons laughed, amused at the request. "Do I look that stupid?"

"Well, kind of," Mia joked.

"Sorry, lady. You and your friend are going to be joining your other friend in a few minutes. By the way, who is this guy?" Simmons wondered.

"Just a friend."

"You sure have a lot of friends who are gonna turn up dead."

"You don't think we came up here without telling anyone, did you?" Mia asked, hoping to delay what she hoped wasn't inevitable.

"You're lying."

Mia shrugged.

"Who'd you tell?" Simmons asked, now getting a slight look of concern on his face.

"You'll meet them soon enough. Unless they kill you before you get a chance to see their faces," Mia told him, hoping to get him nervous enough that he'd just leave.

"Sorry, I think I'm better off just blowing the both of your heads off before anyone else arrives and just blowing the scene."

Simmons raised his gun up to Mia's head, about a foot away from her forehead and was about to pull the trigger. Mia closed her eyes, not believing that she was stupid enough to put themselves in that situation. Recker was right, she thought. She wasn't trained in this sort of thing and she wasn't prepared for what might result from her asking questions. If she was going to find her way out of her predicament, she was going to have to think of something fast.

"If you kill me, there's no place on earth that you can hide from him," Mia quickly stated, almost stumbling over her words to get them out before he pulled the trigger.

"From who?" Simmons wondered.

"I told him that I was coming here," she said, breathing heavily as she tried to think.

"Told who?" Simmons angrily asked.

"If I don't make it out of here, there's nowhere that you can go that he won't find you."

"I'm not gonna ask a third time."

"The Silencer," she finally revealed.

Recker's reputation had grown so much that everyone

knew his moniker. Most people thought he did good work, helping those in need. But criminals like Simmons and others of his ilk, had become deathly afraid of hearing his name. Most that had rap sheets, except for the extremely dangerous ones, hoped to never cross paths with him. Simmons could be counted among those that hoped to never find him. Though he was dangerous in his own right, after the countless stories that he'd heard over the past year involving Recker, he wasn't eager to mix it up with him.

"You know The Silencer?" Simmons asked.

Mia hesitated, hearing the worry in his voice as he said the name. "Yes."

"How do you know him?"

"I'm just a friend."

"Just a friend, huh? How do I know you're telling the truth? Maybe you're lying and just saying that," Simmons stated.

"I'm not. He already knows about you."

Simmons didn't seem to be convinced. "Yeah, well, if he knows about me then why isn't he here right now instead of you and the professor looking guy over there?"

"He was attending to something else, and I told him that I could do this and there wouldn't be any problems," Mia explained.

"Looks like you were incorrect on that one," Simmons scoffed.

"Tell me about it."

"Well if he's on my trail, then it doesn't look like I need you either way," Simmons said, raising his gun up again.

"No, please," Mia pleaded. "I can get him to back off you. But I can only do that if we walk out of here alive."

Jones began to stir and noticed that Simmons seemed to be so preoccupied with Mia that he didn't even pay any attention to him. Though he still felt a little groggy and was sure he had a concussion, he knew he had to do something if the two of them were going to walk out of there alive. He reached inside his coat pocket and withdrew the gun he took out of Recker's safe. He quickly pointed it at Simmons and pulled the trigger. Jones had fired too hastily though and didn't take long enough to aim properly. His vision was somewhat blurry, and he had more time than he thought he would. He missed Simmons completely; the bullet lodging into the wall behind him. Simmons ducked and ran over to Jones and kicked the gun out of his hand, then punched him in the face. Jones blacked out again.

With Simmons's back turned towards her, Mia rushed over to him and jumped on his back, hoping to dislodge the gun from his hand. After a brief struggle, Simmons hunched over and flung Mia over his shoulder. She landed hard on the wood floor, the back of her head striking it. She winced in pain as she grasped the back of her head. Simmons took a few steps back to make sure there was a safe distance between him and his two hostages, both of whom were still laying on the floor. He still held his gun out, taking turns at pointing to both of his would-be victims as he contemplated his next move. He wasn't completely sure that the woman in front of him was being honest that she knew The Silencer. But he thought it seemed like an odd thing for someone to blurt out, even one who was in as much trouble as she was. If she really did know him, and he killed her, Simmons knew he was as good as dead. But, if he were to take them with him to find out the truth, and they did know him, then Simmons could trade their lives for his own personal safety. And if it turned out that they didn't know The Silencer, then he could kill them at a later time. After a couple more minutes debating with himself the merits of both killing them, or taking them with him, he finally decided on what action to take.

"All right, get up," Simmons said.

Mia did as instructed and slowly got to her feet, thinking both her and Jones were as good as dead. She was a bit surprised when Simmons told them he was taking them with him.

"Get your friend up too," Simmons told her.

"He needs medical attention," Mia replied.

"He'll be fine. Whatever he needs, you can do it."

"What are you gonna do with us now?"

"I'm gonna take you with me for now. If you really do know The Silencer, then you're gonna call him and you're gonna get him off my trail," Simmons informed her.

"Well you already smashed my phone so I can't call him."

"What about his?"

Mia knelt and searched through Jones' pockets but couldn't find his phone anywhere. She thought she saw him with it but couldn't be sure of where it went to.

"I can't find it," Mia told him.

"Whatever. We don't have time right now anyway," Simmons said. "Cops are probably gonna be here soon enough. Someone probably heard that shot and called it in. We have to get going."

"So where are you taking us?"

"I'm gonna take you to a place nobody else knows about. Then you're gonna contact your friend. Wake your friend up and get him on his feet. And you better not be lying to me or else I'll kill you on the spot."

6

Recker didn't stop worrying about what Jones and Mia were doing, especially since he didn't know the exact specifics. That sinking feeling in the pit of his stomach that told him something was wrong only intensified as the time rolled by. He glanced at his phone just as the time changed to one o'clock. He started fidgeting around as he contemplated what he wanted to do. Either Jones or Mia should've checked in with him by now. With his experience, he'd attended several of these informant meetings and he never had one that lasted this long. Even if someone was late, it should've only lasted five, or ten minutes tops.

Recker now had a dilemma. Did he stay and wait for Edwards to show up? Or did he forget about him and head back to Philadelphia to check on his friends? If Jones and Mia were in trouble, they would need every second of his time that Recker could give. If Edwards didn't show up for another five or six hours, that was precious time that he wasn't sure his friends had enough of. After a few minutes of thought, there was no other decision for him to make. Even if he got back to Philadelphia and found his friends were safe, he now knew where Edwards lived. He could always come back. And if the unthinkable happened, and his friends were no longer among the living, finding and killing Edwards would be the only thing he had left.

Before leaving, he tried calling Jones' phone a couple times. He then sent him a few text messages urging him to let him know they were OK. After five minutes, he turned his attention to Mia's phone. He tried her number a few times, but hers went straight to voicemail. That was an immediate red flag as Recker knew she never turned her phone off. With her position as a nurse, she previously had told him that she never had her phone off unless it was broken somehow. Mia always kept it on in case of an emergency. Even if she was in a setting where the ringer had to be off or something, she just set it to vibrate so she could still be alerted.

Recker put his car in drive and headed back toward the highway. If he hurried, he thought he had a chance to make it back in eleven or twelve hours. But in the middle of the day, there was a good chance he'd hit some traffic on the way. If Jones and Mia were in as much trouble as Recker suspected they were, he was going to need some help before he got back. He picked his phone back up and started making some calls.

"Tyrell, I need a big favor," Recker immediately said.

"Name it."

"There's a couple people I think are in trouble. One of them's the professor."

"OK?"

"They told me they were meeting someone at the Haddix Apartment complex at twelve. They still haven't checked in yet. I get the feeling something's wrong."

"So why don't you just go there yourself?" Gibson asked.

"I'm in Ohio right now. I'm on my way back there but I'm at least ten or twelve hours away."

"Ohio? What the hell you doing down there?"

"A story for another time. Do you think you can go there and check out the place? Do you have the time?" Recker asked.

"For you, yeah, I got the time. Haddix Apartments?"

"Yeah. You familiar with it?"

"Yeah, I been there a few times," Gibson answered.

"Well? What about it? What kind of place is it?"

"There's only two reasons most people go there."

"Which are?"

"You either looking for trouble or you running away from it."

"Crap."

"So if you haven't heard from them... they most likely found it."

"All right. How soon can you get there?" Recker asked.

"Gimme about twenty minutes. What's the room number?"

"217. Call me when you get there."

"Will do."

These were the sorts of scenarios that Recker told Jones about when they first started this operation. No matter how good Jones was with computers, like Recker said, he still needed eyes and ears out on the street. There would be times that you needed contacts, friends, people you trusted to do things that a computer couldn't. As Recker continued to drive, his worst fears were starting to flutter front and center in his mind. He couldn't shake the feeling that at least one, or even both, were dead or badly hurt. The next twenty minutes were probably the second longest of his life. The only other instance in which time seemed to go by so slowly was that night in London after Carrie was killed. In that case, it seemed like time stopped completely. The biggest difference now was that he just didn't know. Usually, the uncertainty of not knowing was almost as bad as the pain of knowing the end result. At least with Carrie, though he never had closure yet, or a sense of finality with her killer still at large, at least he had the knowledge that there was nothing else that could be done to save her. Now, he didn't know whether his friends were alive or dead. And that ate him up just as bad.

Recker kept checking the time, counting down until Gibson called. Once the twenty-minute mark was up, and still no call, Recker started worrying more. He imagined that Gibson walked in on a bloody crime scene. He quickly shook his head, trying to get the visions out of his mind and think more positively. Five more minutes passed by with still no word from Gibson. Recker had never been much of an anxious person. Never seemed to worry about much or let much bother him. But when it came to his friends, he was worried sick. As Recker sped down the road, another five minutes came and went before his phone finally started ringing.

"Tyrell, what took you so long? You said twenty minutes," Recker said.

"Man, you know Philly traffic. Took me like twenty-five minutes just to get here," Gibson responded.

"So what's the situation there? How's it looking?" Recker asked with a lump in his throat, praying he wouldn't get the answer that he feared.

"Place is empty, man."

"Empty?"

"Yeah. I mean, like, real empty. Hardly even looks like somebody lives here. If they do, they must not believe in modern technology or anything."

"Tell me what you see. Any signs of a struggle or a fight or anything?"

Gibson looked around the room but didn't notice anything. "Nah, man. Like I said, there's not even much here to mess up. Even if there was a fight there's no way of knowing."

"Damn," Recker sighed, thinking of his next course of action.

"Hold up, there's a hole in the wall."

"What kind of hole?"

"Like a bullet hole."

"What's near it?"

"Whaddya mean, what's near it?"

"Well is there blood on the wall or floor underneath it?" Recker asked.

"Nah, nothing."

"Whoever shot it must've missed their target then."

"Anything else?"

"Not that I see. Wait a minute, wait a minute," Gibson stated, walking to the other side of the room and looking more closely at the floor and wall where Jones had been propped up.

"What is it?"

Gibson knelt by the wall and touched the red mark on the floor with his finger to analyze it. "It's blood, man."

"You notice anything else? Maybe something that was dropped by mistake, or even on purpose? Anything that seems out of place?"

"No, like I said, there ain't much here to begin with," Gibson answered, moving throughout the apartment just to double check.

"The only thing you see is the blood?" Recker asked.

"Yeah, that's it."

"How much is it? Like someone got shot?"

"Uh, no, I don't think so. It's not like a big pool or anything, more like a couple drips here or there. More like someone got busted up in the head or something. Maybe even the hand."

"Thanks Tyrell."

"No problem. I don't know what it was, but something went down here. What's the name of the dude that lives here, anyway?"

"Professor told me the name was Joe Simmons," Recker replied.

"Joe Simmons," Gibson repeated. "Joe Simmons."

"You don't know him, do you?"

"I dunno. For some reason that name rings a bell. Like I heard of him somewhere before."

"Well think. There's two lives that are hanging in the balance here."

"I'm thinking, I'm thinking."

"Yeah, well, while you're doing that, check one more thing for me?" Recker wondered.

"Depends."

"Check the parking lot and see if their cars are there?"

Since it was such a simple request, Gibson agreed and left the room to head down to the parking lot. Recker let him know the makes of Jones' and Mia's car along with the license plate numbers. Once Gibson got down to the lot and spent a few minutes checking, he spotted Jones' car. He walked behind the car and looked at the license plate, getting a match.

"I know you won't like this, but I got the professor's car here," Gibson revealed.

"What about the other one?"

Gibson walked past a few more cars then stopped, noticing a car that fit the description that Recker gave him. He went to the rear of the car and read the plate number, once again getting a match.

"There's number two," Gibson stated.

"You found it?"

"Yeah. Both here."

"Anything unusual? Unlocked, blood, anything?" Recker wondered.

"No. Both locked up tight. No sign of anything else."

"So that means they were both taken somewhere."

"That's a good sign," Gibson replied. "Means they're probably still alive. Otherwise they would've just killed them upstairs."

"Unless they killed them and were dumping the bodies somewhere."

"That's a lot of work to go through all that."

"If it's the person I think we're dealing with, then they got the history of it," Recker said.

"Whatcha mean?"

"I think they might've been meeting the person that killed that girl we found stuffed in the trunk a few months ago."

"Oh man. That's bad news then."

"I know. Anything else on the name? Remember where you heard it before?" Recker asked.

"Nah, I just can't place it. I know I never did business with him before directly or else I'd remember that," Gibson answered. "But I feel like I met him before somewhere. Maybe he was in a group and I remember the name but he wasn't like a main player."

"Well if that's the case then who would you have met in a group that would have someone like that involved?"

"Well, if I'm actually remembering right, then there's only two guys that would have a crew in a group setting that I'd have done business with."

"Let me guess... Vincent or Jeremiah?"

"That's it."

"If this is the guy we're looking for, sounds like an MO that he learned working for Vincent," Recker said.

"How you figure?"

"People that fell victim to Vincent or his crew don't always turn up at the same spot that they were killed. Sometimes they get moved or staged to a different area for whatever reasons. Jeremiah doesn't usually stage his killings. He'll just leave them where they fall."

"Yeah, yeah, that's right. Like, um, that Italian dude that shot you that wound up in that alley a few months back," Gibson said.

"Yeah."

"If Simmons's really part of Vincent's crew, I don't know how happy he's gonna be if you wind up taking him out."

"Let me worry about that."

"You need me to do anything else?"

"Not unless you can find out where Simmons might've gone," Recker responded.

"I mean, I can put some feelers out and see what happened, but I can't really promise much from that."

"Yeah, do what you can do. I appreciate it."

"You got it, bro."

As soon as he hung up, Recker knew what he had to do. He'd have to call Vincent and explain the situation and ask for another favor. Having to ask Vincent to do another thing for him wasn't the ideal scenario. Recker knew that at some point, he was going to have to repay the favors that Vincent had done for him. And however it was that Vincent wanted him to repay those favors, it wasn't likely to be something that Recker would like doing, but he would have no choice but to do it. Regardless of that, Recker didn't have any other options left. He'd have to worry about everything he owed Vincent at a later time.

There also was a different problem that occurred to Recker. And that was if Vincent was somehow involved in the disappearance of Jones and Mia. He was sure that Vincent had no idea that they were friends of his, but the thought crossed his mind, what if for some reason Vincent ordered the killing of Susan Hanley? Recker couldn't wrap his head around why a mob boss would want someone like her killed, but he'd seen and heard of stranger things before. If that was true, then he would have also been responsible for Jones and Mia's situation right now.

If Vincent had Simmons kill the Hanley woman, and Mia somehow uncovered information that indicated such, then she'd be directly in his crosshairs. Even though it all made sense, and it certainly seemed plausible, it was still a big leap to make. Recker still wasn't sure how Hanley would be connected to Vincent to make that big of a conclusion. He figured he'd have to call and gauge Vincent's reaction to what he told him. If Vincent denied Simmons worked for him, or that he had no knowledge of anything and played dumb, then that would indicate that Vincent was involved. But if Vincent acknowledged that Simmons was one of his guys, and he seemed concerned about what was going on, then perhaps everything was being done without his knowledge.

Either way, Recker was going to have to call Vincent to find out. If he wasn't working against a time deadline, and his two friends weren't missing, then there might've been another way around it. Recker could've found out in a more discreet manner than by alerting someone he wasn't sure was innocent or not. But that wasn't the situation he found himself in and he'd just have to take his chances. The one good thing about his past dealings with Vincent was that Recker now had a direct line of communication with him. He didn't have to go through third parties or other sources to get into contact with Vincent quickly. And while he didn't have Vincent's personal number, he had Malloy's, and considering he was his right-hand man and almost always by his side, it basically amounted to the same thing. He dialed the number as he drove, getting through on the second ring.

"Recker," Malloy cautiously answered. "What can I do for you?"

"I need to talk to your boss."

"What about?"

"It's urgent," Recker answered.

"You're gonna have to do better than that."

Not wanting to reveal specifics yet, Recker thought of a generic answer while still conveying the general tone of the message. "There's a couple cases I've been working on and I need to know whether he's involved or not before I know how to proceed."

"He's not readily available right now," Malloy stalled.

"Well get him available. Cause if he's not, and one of his men is responsible for what I'm working on, then he's gonna have to worry about getting a new guy. Cause this one's gonna be dead."

Sensing the seriousness of the situation, Malloy dropped the stall tactics and thought it best to get his boss on the line. "Hold on."

It didn't even take thirty seconds before Vincent got on the other end of the phone. "Mike, what can I help you with?"

"I need answers. And I need the truth."

"Well I'll tell you what I can depending on the specifics of the question," Vincent replied, not sounding the least bit concerned or bothered.

"There was a woman doctor who was killed about three months ago," Recker explained. "She was found stuffed in the trunk of a car which was found near the airport. Do you know anything about that?"

Vincent took a few seconds to genuinely think about the question. "I seem to recall hearing something about that though I don't know too much of the specifics. Why do you ask?"

"I've been close to finding out the killer and I think he works for you. I need to know if you were involved and if the order came from you," Recker told him.

"It did not," Vincent quickly replied. "If it was someone who works for me, then it was done without my knowledge or consent."

"Which leads me to my next problem. Two more people, civilians, friends of this woman, started looking into her death on their own time."

"Let me guess... they're now in trouble?"

"They found this guy that I was looking at and now they're both missing," Recker said.

"And you're wondering if I'm involved in the death of this woman and the disappearance of her friends."

"That's pretty much it."

"Considering it's you who's asking, I'll help you out with your problem," Vincent stated. "If it was anybody else, I wouldn't give them the time of day."

"Understood."

"I will tell you with complete honesty and the utmost respect that what's happened, or happening, to these people... I have nothing to do with."

"Then that's good enough for me. I accept you for your word."

"Good. Now that that's out of the way, you said you were looking for someone who you believe is part of my crew. I'm assuming you have a name."

"I do. The name is Joe Simmons," Recker revealed.

Vincent did not immediately respond as he recognized the name instantly. He let it sink in for a minute before responding. With Vincent's hesitation, Recker assumed that he was familiar with the name.

"Considering you didn't immediately say that you had no idea who he is, I take it that you do know him," Recker said.

Vincent took another moment to respond. "Yes, Joe Simmons is one of my men."

Neither Recker nor Vincent knew what else to say after that revelation and both stayed silent for a minute.

Vincent's curiosity then took hold, wondering what Recker was planning on doing.

"How exactly do you plan to proceed now with that knowledge?" Vincent asked.

"I plan to proceed and find Joe Simmons. He doesn't happen to be with you now, is he?"

"He is not. He is called when he's needed."

"Oh."

"And if or when you do find him? What then?"

"There's a good chance I'm gonna kill him," Recker answered. "Is he a high-ranking member of your organization that you'd object to that?"

"No. He's a grunt man. He's usually used for things that might involve a little muscle. He's not involved in day-to-day matters."

"Then you won't have a problem with me killing him."

"Are you asking for my blessing in killing one of my men?" Vincent wondered.

"I just want to make sure we don't have any problems or issues that arise out of this."

Vincent took a few more seconds to think before responding, getting a little more angry about the situation, though he didn't let it show. "We will not. I'll do you one better."

"What's that?" Recker asked.

"We'll find Joe Simmons for you."

"I'm not asking you to do that."

"You don't have to. If he's done these things as you suggest he has then he's operating without my knowledge or approval on these matters," Vincent tersely stated. "And if that's the case then he's defying my wishes and orders."

"So you'll make an example out of him?"

"Think of it as you wish. Sometimes those in positions of power must do things that will shock and awe in order to keep the rest of the herd inline."

"Well that's up to you. My main interest is getting these innocent people back safe and sound," Recker replied.

"We both have our own motives for finding him. It might help to know where you think these people have been or where they were taken."

"I believe they were taken at the Haddix Apartments. Simmons had a room there."

"I know the place. He had a room there that he used as a front in order to conduct some business dealings," Vincent explained. "When did all this occur?"

"They were supposed to meet with him about twelve," Recker answered.

"I assume you've already been there."

"I'm currently out of state. I was working on another case but I'm on my way back now. I had someone check the apartment though and there's no one there."

"I'll have someone check his home, though I'm fairly certain he wouldn't have taken them there."

"Where would he go?"

"There's a few places I can think of. How far away are you?"

"Probably about ten or twelve hours," Recker replied.

"Don't rush. We'll find him."

"What am I gonna owe you?"

"We'll talk about it another time," Vincent responded. "Let's accomplish our goal first. Once we locate him, we'll give you a call."

Recker was relieved in some fashion. At least he now knew that Vincent wasn't involved in anything, but he wouldn't feel total relief until he knew both Jones and Mia were safe and unharmed. Though he had total confidence in Vincent's ability to find his employee, he still worried about whether he'd find Simmons before he did something stupid. Once Vincent ended the conversation with Recker, he turned to his right-hand man to get the manhunt started.

"We're looking for Joe Simmons?" Malloy asked, overhearing the conversation.

"Yes."

"What for? What'd he do?"

"Recker believes he killed some doctor a few months ago and stuffed her in a trunk by the airport," Vincent explained.

"So?"

"Recker also believes her friends went looking for answers and ran into Joe a little over an hour ago and haven't been heard from since."

"Excuse me for saying so, boss, but what's that got to do with us? I mean, so what? What do we care?" Malloy wondered.

"Our reasons for caring are twofold," Vincent replied. "One, as a favor to Recker to further deepen our relationship and foster goodwill between us. As I've said before, the day will come when perhaps his services will be useful to us. And when it comes, he'll remember times like these when we helped him."

"And second?"

"Secondly, I gave explicit orders months ago that everyone was to lay low and not do anything without my orders or permission. Not one person under my command has the authority to kill anyone without my say so," Vincent angrily stated.

"I know."

"Killing is dangerous business. Kill the wrong person, at the wrong time, make careless mistakes, things have a way of unraveling and coming back to you. Unless it's under self-defense, killing is not something that's to be done haphazardly. If it's found out by the law or the public that Joe killed that woman, and then he kidnapped or killed these two people today... that's bad for our business. They'll find out his connection to me and bring unwanted attention to our operation."

"Understood," Malloy said.

"Besides all that, Joe's a minor player in our business. As I explained to Recker, sometimes examples need to be made to show that insubordination will not be tolerated or allowed. If it was someone more important in our day-to-day operations, perhaps we'd be more calculated on our decisions or even let it slide. But under the circumstances, we'll use this to further cement that my authority is not to be willfully or carelessly ignored."

7

It'd been roughly an hour since Recker and Vincent's conversation. Immediately after, Vincent sent teams of his men out into the city, scouring different buildings in search of finding Joe Simmons. Since Simmons was one of the low men on the totem pole in Vincent's business, he didn't always have steady employment from the mob boss, so he often did several things of the illegal variety on the side.

Simmons knew that if The Silencer was on his tail like Mia suggested, then he couldn't go back to his own home. He took his prisoners to a vacant one story building in the northeast part of the city that used to house several different offices. Simmons tied them each to a chair and separated them, placing them in different rooms.

"What's his phone number?" Simmons asked.

"I'm not telling you," Mia replied.

"If you value your life, you'll tell me. Otherwise, I'm

just gonna wind up killing the both of you now and take my chances with him."

"That would be foolish."

"Yeah, well, wouldn't be the first time I did that.."

She was kicking herself for the situation she was now in. Not only did she put her own life in danger, she put Jones' life in jeopardy as well. In addition to that, she knew she was going to put Recker in a tough position in regards to how he was going to handle Simmons. Not to mention the fact that she felt he was going to be furious with her for making him drop whatever he was doing to come rescue her. Mia was so mad at herself that for a brief moment she felt like she deserved whatever Simmons had planned for her. Simmons took his phone out and held it out for Mia to see.

"The number?" Simmons asked again.

Mia tilted her head back, and looked away as she revealed Recker's phone number to him. Simmons gave her an evil glare, not sure she was giving him the right information.

"It better be right," Simmons told her. "If it's not, I'm not trying again."

"It's right," Mia huffed.

The number started dialing and Recker picked up after the second ring. Not recognizing the number, Recker had hoped it was one of Vincent's crew calling him with information that they'd uncovered about Simmons's whereabouts.

"Yeah?" Recker greeted.

"Is this The Silencer?"

"Who's this?"

"I have the pleasure of having two people in my company right now," Simmons answered. "I'm told they're somewhat important to you."

"You're Joe Simmons."

"That's right."

"Are they OK?" Recker asked.

"They're fine for now. You're one friend has a few knots in his head but he'll survive for the moment."

"So what do you want?"

"The girl here told me that you were on my trail," Simmons responded. "I'm willing to do some business with you."

"What do you want?" Recker repeated.

"I'll trade their lives for mine."

"How's that?"

"I'll let them go with the assurance that you forget about me," Simmons offered.

"What makes you think I can or will do that?"

"If you don't, then they're as good as dead."

"And if I agree, what makes you think I won't still come after you?"

"Because I've looked in their wallets and seen their ID's. I know who they are, and I know where they live. You come after me, I go after them," Simmons told him. "I'll even leave the city. I just want your word that you'll let me go and won't come after me."

Fearing the alternative, Recker felt he didn't have any other options but to agree to Simmons's terms. It was actually a good offer as it's probably one that Recker would've offered anyway if it meant getting his friends back unharmed. But the fact that Simmons came up with it right away and without any other strings attached basically made it a no-brainer for Recker to accept the terms.

"Well?" Simmons wondered.

"I'll agree to your conditions," Recker said. "On one condition."

"What's that?"

"I need to hear that they're still alive."

"What? Don't you trust me?"

"Not really."

"I wouldn't try to pull a fast one on you. I know you'd just come after me if I did," Simmons replied.

"I want to hear them," Recker persisted.

"Fine."

Simmons looked at Mia and put the phone up to her ear for her to talk to her friend.

"Say something," Simmons told her.

"I'm so sorry. I'm so sorry for putting you through this," Mia sobbed.

"It's alright. It's OK. I'm gonna get you out of there," Recker replied. "Does this guy know my name?"

"No, no."

"OK, good. Are you and David OK?"

Mia sniffled but kept herself together. "Yeah. Yeah, we're OK."

"All right, that's enough of that," Simmons interjected. "Everyone's OK for now."

"All right. Let them go and you have my word I won't come after you."

"Well, I'm not exactly that trusting of you either."

"What do you mean by that?" Recker asked.

"I'm not gonna just let both of them go and then hope you'll live up to the deal. I'll let one of them go now. The other I'll take with me until I'm out of the city. Once I'm out, I'll put them on a train or a bus back here."

"That's not what I just agreed to."

"Well I'm changing the deal."

"I'm not comfortable with that," Recker objected.

"Either that's the deal or I can just put a couple bullets in their heads right now and take my chances."

"If you do that, I will hunt you down until the ends of the earth. There is no place you can hide from me."

"I release one now and the other I'll send back," Simmons insisted. "Or else."

Recker just shook his head, not liking the new terms. He wasn't in much of a position to bargain though. Agreeing was his only option. "Fine. Release the girl."

Simmons just laughed. "Yeah, I knew you'd say that. No chance. She comes with me."

"Why?"

"Cause she's better company," he teased.

"Fine," Recker said, getting angrier by the minute.

There was no way Recker was just going to let Simmons take Mia out of the city and hope that he was a man of his word and send her back. Recker was going to find him before he got out of the city limits.

"So we have a deal?" Simmons asked.

"Yeah."

"I'll leave your man Jones here tied up for you. And

just in case you decide that since I won't be here with him that you can just come after me first, I'm gonna make sure that's not a wise move."

"What's that supposed to mean?" Recker wondered.

"I've planted an explosive in the room that he's in. If he's still sitting there in an hour... well then, I guess he's gonna go boom," Simmons said with a laugh.

"You're bluffing."

"Maybe I am. Maybe I'm not. You really can't afford to find out though, can you?"

"You've got one hour to get your friend out of here or else this building will explode," Simmons warned.

"You gotta give me the address."

"It's a vacant office building on Knights. You find it."

Simmons then hung up and Recker shouted an expletive as he tossed the phone down on the front seat beside him. He obviously couldn't get there in an hour. He had two options at that point. Tyrell or Vincent. Since he was part of Vincent's crew, Recker figured he might've had an idea of what building he was talking about. He quickly picked his phone back up and dialed Vincent's number.

"What's up?" Malloy answered.

"Is Vincent there?"

Malloy immediately handed the phone over to his boss. "What can I do for you, Mike?"

"I just got a call from Simmons," Recker revealed.

"Oh?"

"He's holding them in a vacant office building somewhere on Knights. Have any idea where he's talking about?"

Vincent thought for a second and seemed to think he might have known where Simmons was. "Yeah, I might have an idea. There's a couple places there that could fit the bill."

"There's complications."

"There usually are," Vincent replied.

"He agreed to let the two people go if I agreed to let him out of the city," Recker told him.

"And your reply?"

"I didn't have much choice but to agree. But he's taking the girl with him and said when he's out of the city he'll send her back."

"And you don't believe him?"

"I'm skeptical."

"As well you should be."

"The guy, he's leaving there for me. But he said if I'm not there in an hour, the room he's in is gonna explode. He said he planted an explosive that'll go off in one hour," Recker explained.

"And you obviously won't be able to get there in time to save him," Vincent stated.

"Yeah."

"Say no more. We'll take it from here."

"Are you sure?"

"No need for you to worry about it anymore. It's my problem now. Your two victims will be safe and sound and Joe's not going to take anyone out of the city."

"What are you gonna do?" Recker wondered.

"That's for me to figure out. Enjoy your drive back, no need to rush and risk getting pulled over by state police or anything," Vincent said with a smile. "I'll only call you if there's an unforeseen problem. If you don't hear from me, assume everything's gone well."

"Uh... all right."

"Call me when you get back in town and we'll arrange a meeting."

"OK. I'll do that. Thanks."

"Don't mention it."

Recker wasn't sure how to feel anymore. Part of him felt like he should be relieved that Vincent assured him that he'd take over the situation from there and make sure everyone was unharmed. But part of him was still a little nervous and anxious as he was basically putting his trust, and the lives of Jones and Mia, in the hands of a crime lord. And even though Vincent had proved trustworthy in all their dealings up to that point and never gave Recker reason to doubt anything he ever told him, he was still the head of a criminal organization. No matter what, Recker was still going to worry until he saw that his two friends were safe. Or at the least heard their voices.

Vincent handed the phone back to Malloy and started to discuss their plans moving forward. Vincent was not about to let Joe Simmons out of the city. Hearing what Simmons's intentions were only affirmed to Vincent that he was making the right decision in helping Recker. If Simmons really was threatening to blow up the building one of his prisoners was in, and he was intent on taking the girl out of town with him, it was an indication to Vincent that the man was becoming unhinged. That was a lot of carnage and destruction, along with heat from law enforcement, that he wasn't authorized to unleash.

"Joe's become unglued," Vincent said. "He's threatening to take the girl out of town and blow up a building with the other guy he took if Recker's not there in an hour."

"So what do you wanna do?" Malloy asked.

"We won't let this drag on any longer. Call him and find out where he is. We'll come to him."

Malloy nodded and started dialing Simmons's number. Every time they had tried to call him previously, the call just went to his voicemail. Now they knew he was avoiding their calls and since he just called Recker, they knew his phone had to be on. Malloy kept trying but to no avail. Simmons just wasn't picking up. Vincent nodded and put his hand up for Malloy to stop trying, indicating it was OK. Vincent got out his own phone and started dialing Simmons's number. It was rare for Vincent to call any of his own men personally. It was usually Malloy that acted as the intermediary. All of Vincent's men were programmed that if he called them personally, it was extremely important, and they needed to pick up the phone immediately or else there would be consequences for them ignoring his call. After the third ring, Simmons finally picked up his phone, mostly out of fear of what would happen to him if he didn't answer his boss' call.

"Joe, we've been trying to call you for a while now," Vincent told him.

"Sorry boss, I was just in the middle of a few things."

"Oh? Anything I need to know about?"

"No, no. Nothing important. Just trying to square some things away. Did you need me for something?" Simmons worriedly asked.

"Well, as a matter of fact, that brings me to why I called," Vincent calmly stated. "I've heard some rumblings that are terribly concerning to me."

"What's that?"

"I've been told that right now you're holding two people against their will inside a vacant office building on Knights Road. Is that correct?"

"Umm...," Simmons stumbled, not wanting to lie to his leader in fear of what would happen if he did. But he also didn't want to admit the truth and have to explain himself.

"You don't have to say anything. I already know where you're at and who's with you."

Simmons took a big gulp, afraid of what he was going to hear next.

"I've also heard that you're responsible for the killing of some female doctor that was found in the trunk of a car by the airport a few months back. Is that correct?" Vincent asked.

"Mr. Vincent, I can explain."

"I don't want explanations, Joe. I also don't want apologies. It's too late for both of those things."

"I'm sorry."

"Mr. Vincent, The Silencer's on my trail, I'm just trying to somehow stay ahead of him," Simmons said.

"The Silencer, huh?"

"Yes, sir."

"What are your plans right now?" Vincent asked.

Even though Vincent already knew the situation, he was trying to play coy to get Simmons's guard down. If Simmons suspected that Vincent was also gunning for him, he'd leave town in a split second. Of course, Vincent believed he could track him down if need be, but it'd take a lot more work than planned and more effort than what he thought was necessary. It'd be much easier to bring Simmons in if he believed that Vincent was on his side. Simmons then explained the situation to his boss, telling him about his plans, his deal with Recker, even the explosive that he had planted.

"I'll tell you what, Joe. I want you to stay put and don't do anything for right now," Vincent told him.

Simmons stuttered at first, nervous about staying there with Recker on the way. "But I, uh, I... I don't know if I can handle him on my own."

"Just listen to what I tell you and you'll be fine. I'm going to send Jimmy and some other boys with him to your location. We'll set a trap for The Silencer when he gets there and we'll take him out for you. That way you never have to worry about him again and you don't have to think about leaving town."

"Mr. Vincent, thank you. Thank you. I appreciate your help," Simmons replied.

"No problem, Joe. I just wish you would've come to me sooner and we wouldn't have had to go through all this trouble. We'll take care of you though, don't worry."

"Should I get rid of these people first?"

"No. You keep them right where they are. We'll use

them as part of the trap. Just keep them unharmed for now," Vincent answered.

"OK. No problem. When should Jimmy get here?"

"Give him about twenty or thirty minutes."

Simmons then proceeded to give Vincent his location, though the crime boss already had a good idea that that's where he was. Still, it avoided any possibilities of errors and lost time. As soon as Vincent got off the phone, he gave Malloy the address and told him to grab a few of his men so they could leave right away. After his conversation with his boss, Simmons was now feeling pretty confident. Even with Recker's reputation, he didn't think he could match up with all of Vincent's crew just waiting there for him. Simmons then went back into the room where Mia was.

"Looks like a change of plans, sweetheart," he said.

"What?"

"I was originally going to take you with me as an insurance policy but it looks like that won't be necessary."

"Why not? What are you gonna do?" Mia asked.

"I just talked to my boss. He instructed me to stay here and we'll deal with your friend in the appropriate manner."

"You're setting a trap for him?" she worriedly asked.

Simmons just grinned, happy at the change of plans.

"But you made a deal," Mia told him.

"Sometimes things don't work out the way you planned. Just sit tight for a while and it'll all be over soon."

Simmons then took out a white rag and shoved it in

Mia's mouth, wrapping a piece of string around the back of her head to prevent her from talking and warning Recker when he arrived. Once he secured her and made sure she wasn't going anywhere, he left the room to check on his other prisoner. Mia started squirming, struggling to break free of her restraints. She tried wiggling loose, kicking her legs in the air, frantically wanting to get out from her ropes. After a few minutes she knew it was no use. She was locked in tight. Her heart sank as she thought about what Recker was about to walk into. They were being used to get to him. Though she hoped against all hope that Recker could somehow survive and fight his way through whatever obstacles he was up against, she knew it'd be tough sledding for him.

Simmons then went into the other room where Jones was sitting. The professor was sitting quietly and still, knowing that Recker was already somehow on the case. Since he told Recker he'd check in after the meeting, he figured alarm bells were going off once he never contacted him. That and the fact that Mia wasn't answering her phone either, Jones knew that he was either on the way or getting someone there in his place. Jones had a calm expression on his face and Simmons noticed that his prisoner didn't look worried. Unlike Mia, who Simmons could tell was a little upset and worried about what was happening, Jones didn't seem to have the same attitude.

"You seem awfully calm considering what's going on," Simmons stated.

"Worrying isn't going to change or alter whatever happens here," Jones replied.

"That's a very good attitude you have there. You know, in my original plan, I was thinking about putting a bomb in here. Maybe The Silencer would get to you in time, maybe he wouldn't. But there was a very good chance that you might've exploded."

"And that plan has changed?"

"I've got some friends coming. There's no need for me to be cute or play games. We're gonna have a little surprise waiting for your friend when he gets here," Simmons replied.

"You're going to ambush him?" Jones asked.

"That's what the boss wants."

"Boss? So you're not a lone wolf then. Who is your employer?"

"You think I'm dumb enough to tell you that?"

Jones shrugged. "I don't see the harm in it. I'm obviously not escaping from here to tell anyone. And if you succeed in your plan, then after you kill The Silencer, I'm quite certain you'll turn the tables on Ms. Hendricks and me so we can join him. And if you're not successful, then it won't matter because you'll be dead."

Simmons laughed, amused that his prisoner thought there was a chance The Silencer would kill them all. "There's no chance of that happening."

"Well if you're so sure of your plan, then you won't mind explaining it to me. At least give me the satisfaction of having the knowledge of what's about to happen before I go to the grave," Jones told him.

"I work for a man named Vincent."

"Vincent?"

"Yeah. You know him?"

"Well, by reputation only. What's he got to do with this?"

"He says he wants to have a little welcoming party for your friend when he gets here," Simmons said.

"And when is all this going to go down?"

"Your friend has less than an hour."

"And he said he's coming?" Jones wondered.

"Oh, he'll be here. And we'll be waiting."

Finished with their conversation, Simmons left the room to wait for his friends. Jones knew something was up. He obviously was aware that Recker couldn't get there in less than an hour. So he figured that if Recker said he could, then he must've had something planned. Could that plan involve Vincent? Although Jones was a little worried that if Simmons was Vincent's man, perhaps he reconsidered his relationship with Recker. Could be he'd decide that Recker was no longer worth keeping around. With less than an hour to go, at least his mind wouldn't have long to think about it. Whatever was going to happen, would happen soon enough.

8

———————

Simmons rushed over to the front of the building and looked out a window. He thought he heard someone moving out there along with some muffled voices. He worried that Recker might've gotten there a little earlier than expected and before the reinforcements from Vincent arrived. Simmons looked a little to the right, past the front door, and saw a couple of familiar faces. Malloy was leading the pack. It was exactly thirty minutes since Simmons's conversation with his boss and he was sweating it out the whole time until his back up came. He hurried over to the door and unlocked it, opening it for the rest of the crew to come in. Malloy led the way, followed by four others who, judging by the scowls on their faces, didn't look too enthusiastic about being there.

"Was starting to get worried," Simmons told them. "Thought you'd already be here by now."

"We had some things to take care of on the way," Malloy replied.

"Oh. Well no big deal. As long as you beat The Silencer here that's all that really matters."

"So where are they?"

"Who?"

"The two people you're holding."

"Oh, back here."

Simmons led them through the office and down a hallway to show them his two prisoners. Mia was in an office to the left and Jones was in an office to the right directly across from her. They checked in on Mia first. As soon as Malloy saw her with the gag in her mouth, he walked over to her and undid the string that held it in place to remove it.

"What're you doing?" Simmons wondered, perplexed by his behavior.

"I don't think this will be necessary," Malloy said, dropping the rag on the floor.

"You might be sorry about that. She's a feisty one."

"Are you OK, miss?"

Mia moved her jaw around a few times then nodded. "Yeah."

"Is Vincent coming?" Simmons asked.

"He'll be here shortly," Malloy confirmed. "Where's the other guy?"

"What about her?"

"What about her?" Malloy asked.

"Well, undoing the gag, what if she calls out or something to warn The Silencer when he gets here?" he worried.

"I'm sure she won't do anything like that, will you miss?" Malloy asked her.

Mia looked at him with a painful expression and agreed, even if she wasn't sure she actually would comply with the request. "No."

"See, she'll be fine."

Malloy told one of his men to stay in the room by the door to keep an eye on her as Simmons led them across the hallway to see Jones. He then told another of his men to go wait by the front door to keep an eye out for Vincent's arrival.

"Is he not as much trouble?" Malloy wondered, noticing that Jones wasn't as tightly restrained as the girl was.

"Nah. He's pretty mild-mannered," Simmons answered. "He seems resigned to whatever's gonna happen."

Jones recognized Malloy from the photos that he dug up of Vincent's organization for Recker when he was initially checking into them. Since they didn't seem to know who Jones was, in relation to Recker, he just played along like he wasn't familiar with any of them. Another man stayed in the room with him as Malloy and Simmons went out into the main office to wait for their boss. About five minutes later, the front door opened, with Vincent confidently walking in. A sigh of relief crossed Simmons's face, finally feeling like the situation was secure.

"Jimmy, Joe, how's everything looking?" Vincent asked.

"Everything's good," Malloy answered.

"No issues?"

Malloy just shook his head.

"Joe, I have a few more questions for you," Vincent said.

"Sure."

"On the way over here a couple things hit me out of the blue that I didn't initially think about. You talked to The Silencer on the phone, correct?"

"Yeah," Simmons replied.

"How did you get his number?"

"The girl gave it to me."

"And how did she get it?"

Simmons shrugged. "She said she knew him."

"Really?"

Simmons shrugged again. "Yeah. She had it memorized. Said they were friends."

"Well that's interesting. Wouldn't you say Jimmy?"

"Sure is," Malloy responded.

"Let's meet this girl."

"She's back this way," Simmons said, leading them back to the room she was in.

Vincent, Malloy, and Simmons stood just inside the door, looking at the tied up woman. As they continued to stand there, Mia couldn't help but feel she was in a lot of danger. She could tell by the way Simmons stood behind the others that these guys were the ones in charge of the situation now.

"Pretty girl," Vincent stated to anyone who was listening.

Vincent looked around the barren room and noticed a metal folding chair standing up against the wall in the corner. He slowly walked over to it and grabbed it before taking it over to Mia's location and setting it up a few inches away from her. He unbuttoned his coat as he sat down, wanting to have a conversation with her.

"Mia, is that right?" Vincent asked.

"Yes. Are you the one that holds his leash?"

A grin overtook Vincent's face, appreciating her feisty manner. Smiling, he looked over at Malloy and Simmons, the latter of which wasn't as amused by the comment.

"I told you she was a feisty one," Simmons said.

"I understand you know The Silencer. You're friends with him?" Vincent asked.

"I'm not telling you anything," Mia rebuffed.

Vincent made an expression that hinted at his disappointment with her answer. "That's an unfortunate response. You see, I already know that you do. Having his phone number proves that. I don't really need a confirmation from you to acknowledge that."

"Then what are you asking me for?"

"To participate in a truthful and engaging dialogue," Vincent replied. "I abhor people who lie to me. It's something that just gets under my skin and irritates me to no end. When I find people I can talk truthfully with, and feel like we're having an honest conversation, I truly appreciate their candor, even if it doesn't necessarily jive with my own views. I have a certain respect for them and feel that a bond develops between the two parties."

Mia didn't exactly know who the man was that was

sitting in front of her. But there was something cold and dangerous about him. He seemed nice enough, well spoken, obviously had some degree of intelligence. But underneath all that, she could tell there was something that said he could be more ruthless and dangerous than anybody else in that room. Someone that you didn't want to mess with.

Vincent could see that she was having an internal debate as to how she should handle their conversation. He wasn't upset at her lack of trust to that point. Under the circumstances, with her being kidnapped, tied up, and whatever else Simmons had done to her, he understood her hesitancy. But he viewed her as a great resource at trying to understand Recker further. Up to that point, he knew little about Recker. He obviously knew what most people did, what was broadcast on TV, what was written in the papers, along with whatever intel he got off the street. But here sitting in front of him was someone who knew Recker personally. It was his chance to get more information about him. Something other people didn't know. And with luck, he could learn something he could use at another point in time down the road.

"So if I may ask some personal questions, just how close are you two? Friends? Girlfriend? Casual acquaintance?" Vincent wondered.

Mia took a big sigh before she revealed anything, knowing it was probably in her best interest not to dodge any more questions from him. "Uh... we're just friends."

"Nothing more?" Vincent asked, not sure that her response was accurate.

"Nothing more. We're just friends."

"OK. How may I ask did the two of you meet?"

"Um... some of those stories you read about him in the paper... I was one of them," she told him. "I was having problems with an abusive ex-boyfriend and one day Mi... he just showed up."

Vincent smiled, appreciating her resilience and restraint. He could tell that she was still trying not to reveal too much out of loyalty to Recker. It was a trait that he was fond of and one he required in his own men. Before going any further, he looked toward Malloy and nodded for him and Simmons to leave the room. After they did so, Mia started looking a little more nervous, thinking that something was about to happen to her.

"You don't need to play games with me, Ms. Hendricks. I'm fully aware of his name," Vincent said.

"You are?"

"Mike Recker. I've had the pleasure of doing business with Mike on a few different occasions."

"Oh."

"I take it you two have been friends ever since the day he helped you with your problem," Vincent assumed.

"I guess in a way."

"Not so sure?"

Mia shrugged. "I guess I try to be more friends with him than he does with me."

"Keeps you at arm's length, huh?" Vincent asked.

"Yes."

"Smart on his part."

"Why do you say that?" Mia asked.

"A man as dangerous as Mike is, someone who does the things that he does, it makes sense that he wouldn't want anybody to get too close to him. Take yourself for example. Say you two had feelings for each other and got involved, then someone like Joe out there found out about that, that would make you an appealing target to anyone who was trying to either hurt him or avoid him," Vincent explained.

"Oh. Yeah, I guess it would."

"I'm surprised that he'd still interact with you at all. I'd think that after helping you he'd just move on to his next case. Not get involved with anyone."

"I guess I kind of kept after him."

"Tell me, Mary, what is it that you do for a living?"

"Why do you wanna know?"

"Curiosity mostly."

"I'm a pediatric nurse," she told him.

"A nurse, huh?"

"Yes, why?"

"Have you always done that?" Vincent wondered.

"Well, not always. Before that I worked in an ER. But that's what I went to school for."

"I see. Good skill to have around for a man like Mike. Going to the hospital for some type of procedure for someone like him could be pretty dangerous. Never know who might show up."

"What are you getting at?" Mia asked.

"Honestly, I don't really know. I have a theory though. Hear me out and let me know what you think."

"OK."

"Several months ago, I heard Mike got shot. It was actually a man named Mario Mancini that did it. He worked for the Marco Bellomi crime family. Long story short, Mike came to me in hopes of finding Mancini, which we did. Well, I don't know if you know the results of that but both Bellomi and Mancini were widely featured on news telecasts after they turned up dead," Vincent said.

"Why are you telling me all this?"

"Like I said, curiosity. Now, I'm assuming after Mancini shot him, Mike, didn't go to a hospital. A nurse that he has as a friend, though, that might be very helpful indeed if the need should ever arise."

"Must be."

As the two of them were talking, Mia started looking more relaxed, not so uptight. But as the conversation continued, that worried look returned to her face. Vincent was pumping her for information and she could only assume that he was trying to get as much out of her as he could before he killed her. From Vincent's standpoint, he had as much information as he thought he needed. He was quite convinced that he had a good grasp on things. He figured that Recker kept a relationship with her, albeit one from not that close a distance, just in case he ever needed medical help. He thought it was a genius move and frankly one that he expected from someone who had the talents that Recker did.

Without wanting anything else from Mia, Vincent reached into his coat pocket and pulled out a small folding knife. Mia's eyes widened as she saw him remove the lethal instrument, worried that she was about to feel how lethal the object was. Seeing how scared she was becoming, Vincent sought to put her mind at ease. He leaned forward, the knife dangling off his knee.

"You can relax, Ms. Hendricks. I'm not here to hurt you," Vincent said. "You and your friend will be leaving here shortly, both of you unharmed."

Mia scrunched her face, not sure she believed him. If he was being truthful, she certainly didn't understand what was going on. "You're letting us go?"

Vincent nodded his head. "Yes."

"Not that I'm not happy or grateful, but why?"

"You see, Joe works for me, but what he did to your friend, what he's done to you is not something that I condone," he explained. "I don't wish any harm to come to you. You've done nothing wrong that I can see to be in the position you are right now."

"I thought he said you were setting a trap for Mike?"

"Well, I told him what I thought he wanted to hear in order to keep him here with you long enough for me to arrive. As I told you before, Mike and I have done some business dealings before. We have a standing arrangement of some sorts."

"So you're not gonna try and kill him?"

Vincent let out a feeble laugh. "No, trying to kill Mike would be a tall task for anyone regardless of the odds. I value the skills that Mike possesses. A man like him could be very valuable and in demand for someone in my position. Men like that, you just don't get rid of unless it's absolutely necessary. Men like Joe, however, well, they're highly replaceable. You may or may not know that Mike's out of town on business right now and he called me a little while ago and explained the situation. There was obviously no way he could get here in time to save you and your friend so he called me. And I told him I would rectify the situation. And so here we are."

Vincent then took his knife and put it between Mia's ankles and cut the rope that tied them together. He then got up and walked behind her and cut the rope that bound her hands. Once Mia's hands were free, she rubbed her wrists to try to relieve some of the pain from the pressure of the ropes. Vincent walked back in front of her as she began to stand up. Vincent put his arm up to keep her there a few more minutes.

"Am I free to go?" Mia asked.

"I'm going to ask you to remain here a little while longer," Vincent responded. "I first want to talk to the other man that was with you."

"Are you letting him go too?"

"After a brief conversation, yes. I wasn't informed of his name. Perhaps you can save me the trouble of finding out."

"Uh... David."

"David? David what?"

"Uh... Jones."

"Jones, huh?" Vincent asked, not believing that was his real name.

"Yep."

"How do you two know each other?"

"Umm... friend of the family. Yeah," Mia replied, saying the first thing that came to her.

"OK. I'm going to leave a man just outside the door. For your own protection. You're free to walk around in here if you like. I will let you know when it's safe for you to leave. Shouldn't be too long."

Mia nodded, and though she was anxious to go, figured a few more minutes wasn't too much to ask. She was just relieved that she'd be leaving at all considering a half hour previous to that she thought she was on her final breaths.

Vincent walked out of the room and closed the door behind him. He instructed one of his men to just stand there and make sure the woman didn't exit the room. Vincent stood outside the other door, thinking about how he wanted to approach Mia's friend. He took a deep breath, then walked in, grinning, and looking relaxed. Once again, Vincent looked for a chair and found one in the corner of the room. He grabbed it and walked over to Jones, setting it up right in front of him. He then sat down about a foot away as they began to converse.

"So... Mr. Jones," Vincent said. "I've been told you have no identification on you to confirm who you are."

"Sounds as though you already know," Jones replied.

"Courtesy of your lady friend across the hall."

"Is she OK?"

Vincent nodded, "she's fine."

"Am I correct in assuming that you are Vincent?" Jones asked, even though he already knew.

"And how would you know that?"

"Well, your man told me he was waiting for you and seeing as how you have a certain presence about you it would only seem to reason that you are him."

Vincent smiled. "Very astute observation. So is Jones your real name or is it some type of alias that you and The Silencer have worked out?"

"Alias? I'm afraid I don't know what you're talking about."

"So are you telling me you don't know the identity of The Silencer?"

Jones shook his head, hopeful that he wouldn't get tripped up in a lie. "No, I don't. I only know what I read and hear. Nothing more than that."

"So you're telling me that Ms. Hendricks knows The Silencer, you know her, but yet you have no intimate knowledge of him?"

"That is correct. Mia's relationship to The Silencer is no concern of mine and whatever that relationship is... is not my business."

"And yet you accompanied her today. Why?" Vincent wondered.

"While her relationship to The Silencer is not my concern, her safety is. I was concerned about her meeting this man alone and wanted to protect her in any way I could. Obviously that did not work out as well as I would have hoped."

Vincent smiled. "Seems playing the bodyguard isn't really what you're suited for."

"Indeed."

"Exactly what is your business?" Vincent asked.

"I'm a... professor," Jones replied.

He couldn't believe he was actually using the nickname Recker had given him. But, he could see how it might fit in the eyes of other people. And if it helped to get him out of this jam, he'd be more than happy to keep on using it.

"Of what?" Vincent asked.

"History. I teach at Temple."

"So if I call down to Temple, they'll have knowledge of you?"

"Of course," Jones answered, staying strong in his bluff.

Though Vincent still wasn't sure he bought Jones' story, he didn't want to get too in depth with the questions. He was mostly trying to just scratch the surface and get whatever information he could without it sounding like an inquisition.

"So how long have you known Mike Recker?" Vincent asked.

"Who?"

"Mike Recker."

Jones answered with a slight shake of his head. "I'm afraid I don't know the name."

"And you're telling me you've never asked Ms. Hendricks who The Silencer is? Knowing full well that she probably knows his real identity."

"It's not something that really interests me," Jones stated.

"Really? Odd, don't you think?"

Jones shrugged. "I'm not much for conspiracy theories

or unlocking secrets. I believe it's usually best to let things lie as they are. If things are meant to be uncovered they usually will be in due time."

"You're probably right. You're an intellectual man, Mr. Jones. I like that," Vincent grinned.

"Well, I teach so that kind of goes with the job."

"Yes, I suppose so. Not only intellectual, but fascinating."

"I don't think I've said anything that fascinating," Jones responded.

"No, it's not in what you say but how you say it. How you act. How you reply."

A more concerned look overtook Jones' face as he peered up at his visitor. He worried that Vincent had somehow figured out who he actually was. Or he'd already talked to Mia, and she gave him up. Not that he'd blame her if she did as she wasn't the most experienced at this sort of thing. He wouldn't expect her to hold up long against extensive interrogation techniques if she was exposed to them.

"And what makes you think that?" Jones wondered.

"Well, here you are sitting and talking to me calmly and rationally, seemingly knowing full well who I am. And yet you don't look concerned in the slightest," Vincent explained. "You've been beat up, knocked out, kidnapped, tied up to a chair for hours inside a vacant room and yet you don't seem rattled or fidgety. Very strange, wouldn't you agree?"

Jones simply looked down at the floor to the left of him and let a smirk emerge onto his face. He realized that

Vincent was analyzing how he replied to questions more so than the words that Jones used. It was a smooth technique that Jones didn't notice at first.

"I mean, I assume that as a professor you aren't subjected to this type of behavior every week, are you?" Vincent asked.

"I would hope not."

"But you're as cool as can be like it's just another day."

"I guess I'm just a low key type of person where not much bothers me," Jones said.

"Well if this doesn't bother you, I don't know what would."

"Well, would yelling and shouting and trying to break free do me much good?"

"Not really."

"I'm not really sure I understand what you're trying to get at. Are you implying that you think I'm The Silencer?" Jones asked with a laugh.

Vincent chuckled at the suggestion. "Of course not."

"I should hope not. I mean, if I was, I probably wouldn't still be sitting here. James Bond I'm not."

"Wouldn't it be interesting if you were? No, I'm fully aware that you're not The Silencer," Vincent stated.

"May I ask you a couple of questions?" Jones wondered.

"Fire away, professor."

"What is this interest in The Silencer that you have? Do you believe I'm friends with him somehow?"

Vincent got up and walked around the room for a few moments as he pondered the question, giving it ample thought. After a minute, he stopped in back of the metal folding chair where he'd been sitting, leaning on the back of it as he looked down at Jones to answer his questions.

"My fascination with him is I guess the same as almost anyone else's. A vigilante type character who mysteriously shows up in our city... almost like out of a comic book or a movie. When not much is known about someone, you try to figure out their angle, who their associates are, what their play is, what type of connections they have," Vincent explained.

"And you think I may have some of those answers?"

"I'm not sure. And as for friends, I'm not sure a man like The Silencer has friends. I believe he has acquaintances, business partners, perhaps a few people he's friendly with, but men like him, rarely have true friends. They can't afford it."

"Why do you say that?"

"Men who can do the things he does come from a special background. Military, government, black ops, things of that nature. It's rare for a civilian, even one trained in an organization such as mine to be able to move the way he does. He operates in the shadows, in the background, pops up out of nowhere before disappearing, helping people without wanting credit. That's a rare person," Vincent continued.

"I would have to take your word for it. I've never met someone of that background."

"That's why they don't have friends. They pick up and move at the slightest hint of trouble or of being detected. Once they're compromised, they are no longer effective.

It's tough to pack up and move if you're leaving behind people you care about."

"It's a fascinating discussion but not one in which I can be of much value in, considering I have no experience in it," Jones replied.

The longer they talked, the more Vincent was convinced that Jones wasn't merely just a professor as he proclaimed. Vincent thought there was something else there. Perhaps he was a professor. But for a man sitting there tied up, something in which Vincent had a lot of experience, Jones didn't appear anxious, nervous, or fearful. Vincent had many men in that position, some of whom were dangerous in their own right, and all of them showed some type of reaction while in that chair. But not Jones. A professor who didn't exhibit one negative reaction to being there sent red flags into the air in Vincent's mind. Vincent put his hand up in the air, indicating he had more to bring to the discussion.

"I have one final thing on the subject," Vincent told him.

"OK?"

"It's my belief that a man like The Silencer can't really operate on the kind of scale that he has been without some type of help or guidance."

"Really? You mean he has a team?" Jones asked.

"In a way. Like Ms. Hendricks, a nurse who could help him in the event he's ever shot. Perhaps he has a computer genius who works magic for him..."

"Or even an intelligent professor who can help solve problems for him," Jones interrupted.

"Perhaps."

"That is an interesting theory."

"What do you think?" Vincent asked. "As a professor, do you think my theory holds any weight?"

Making a few faces as he feigned thinking about it, Jones concurred. "I believe it's possible, yes."

The conversation came to a halt and the two men just stared at each other for a minute, each apparently sizing the other one up. Jones was obviously a very intelligent man who wasn't going to be rattled or slip up in his story. Vincent didn't want to push too far as he knew that if the man before him was in The Silencer's stable, that he'd tell Recker about the questions and suspicions he had. And while Vincent sought to extract more information about Recker and his operation, he didn't want to push the boundaries just yet and risk making a new enemy. Especially when up to that point they'd had a good relationship.

"If you're done with the assertions, can I ask what you're planning on doing to us?" Jones wondered, breaking the silence after a couple of minutes.

"You will be released, Ms. Hendricks and yourself."

"Thank you."

"I would like to ask one thing of you, though," Vincent said.

"Oh?"

"As a professor, a law-abiding man as I'm sure you are, I'm asking that you don't report any of what's happened here today to the police. It'll be dealt with."

"Well, that goes against my principles," Jones

expressed, trying to keep up his appearances. "I mean, the man did commit several serious crimes. How do I know he won't try again at some point? I don't want to be walking to class every day in fear that he's behind me, ready to strike or something."

"I give you my word that he'll never be an issue for you again. As I said, his crimes will be dealt with," Vincent sternly replied. "Not by a court of public opinion, though, and not by the law. It'll be dealt with by my law. And I assure you that that is far more severe."

9

Once Vincent had finished up with his interview of Jones, he had untied him and assured him he'd be leaving soon, just as he had with Mia. He still left a guard there between the two rooms even though both doors were locked. Vincent then walked out into the main part of the vacant office, ready to conclude the business they had there. Malloy looked at his boss, ready to take action once he got the word.

"Jimmy, once we all go, I want you to stay back and let Ms. Hendricks and Professor Jones out," Vincent ordered.

"You got it."

"If they need a lift or a ride anywhere, take them wherever they'd like to go."

"Right," Malloy replied.

"Wait, what?" Simmons asked, his face a picture of wide-eyed, wide-mouthed astonishment. "You're letting them go?!"

"That's right, Joe," Vincent confirmed.

"What am I missing here? They came looking for me."

"No, I'm fairly certain that whatever happened here today has come to a satisfactory conclusion."

"They're not gonna stop," Simmons objected. "They know The Silencer. I'm as good as dead if he comes after me. They're leverage for me."

"No, Joe, this ends today," Vincent repeated, nodding at Malloy.

Malloy immediately lunged at Simmons and gave him a thunderous right hook across the side of his left cheek. Simmons was surprised and stunned by the blow and instantly fell to the ground. Knowing he was in a world of trouble, he started to get back to his feet. His progress was halted though as the two men that were guarding the door rushed over to him and grabbed each of his arms as they held him in check. As Simmons was dragged back up off the floor, Malloy proceeded to rain down some more punishment on him. Blow after blow, alternating between the stomach, kidneys, and his face, it wasn't long before Simmons was in excruciating pain. As Malloy continued his assault, Vincent stepped forward, speaking to their victim as he was getting hammered with fists.

"You see, Joe, this was necessary because you put my organization in a bad light," Vincent told him. "Your actions made this a necessity because you compromised my positions."

"I'm sor...," Simmons tried to reply.

He couldn't get the rest of the words out, though, as Malloy popped him right across the jaw. With every punch, the pain that Simmons felt increased tenfold. Vincent let the action continue for a few more minutes until he felt satisfied in his own mind that Simmons had successfully gotten the message.

"You killed some female doctor that you had a crush on, or rejected you, doesn't really matter which. I gave explicit directions months ago that nobody was to be killed by one of my men in this city unless it was under my direct orders," Vincent explained to him. "Then her friends come looking for you and you kidnap them with the intention of killing them, bringing The Silencer into the equation. Did you really think I would be OK with that?"

Unable to answer with Malloy still using Simmons as a punching bag, Vincent took hold of his lieutenant's right arm. He gave Malloy a few pats on the back to indicate he was appreciative of his efforts on a job well done. Vincent, along with his men, stood over their former colleague as he writhed around in pain, coughing and spitting up blood.

"I just..." Simmons huffed, trying to catch his breath.

It felt like one or two of his ribs were fractured and he had numerous cuts on his face. His lip was busted, one of his eyes was already starting to swell up, and his nose was broken. He barely had any breath left within him to talk.

"I just," Simmons coughed. "Wasn't think... thinking," he struggled to say, spitting up more blood on the floor.

"Obviously," Vincent responded.

Malloy stood there, ready to pounce on their victim again if he was given the instructions to do so. He looked at his boss to see if he wanted him to continue pounding away, but Vincent didn't give him the green light. Instead, Vincent just stared down at the incredibly beaten man with a look of scorn and contempt. Eventually, Vincent looked over to his right-hand man and could tell that he was still itching to dish out some more punishment.

"I think our friend here has had enough, Jimmy, don't you think?" Vincent asked.

"Whatever you say, boss."

"Take him to the car."

Two of Vincent's men scraped Simmons off the floor again, carrying him out the door and into the car that was waiting for them. Once they had gone, Vincent took Malloy's arm and led him to the far wall to discuss things further without anyone overhearing.

"Take them wherever they want to go and stay on them," Vincent told him. "Perhaps one of them goes somewhere that could give us some additional intel on where Recker sets up shop."

"Why the extra interest in Recker's activities and operations?"

"Keep your enemies close, Jimmy. Keep your friends closer. Right now he's an ally. As we both know, allegiances have a tendency to shift from time to time depending on which way the wind blows. If that should ever happen, it's best to be prepared for a worst-case scenario. And he's a man in which you need disaster plans to be made ahead of time, before the tornado strikes."

"OK. What if these two split up somewhere?" Malloy asked.

Vincent looked over to the hallway that led to both rooms that their visitors were in and debated the question. "If that happens, follow the professor. I think he's a little bit shiftier than she is. I think she was pretty much honest about her relationship with Recker. Him, on the other hand, he's a different story. I think there's much deception about him."

"I'll stay on him. What about Recker?"

"I'll call our friend in a little while and inform him that the matter's been settled. Not until you've done your part, though."

Vincent then left, followed by the man that was guarding the doors, leaving just Malloy with their two guests. Malloy waited a minute until Vincent and the rest of his crew had driven off before he let Mia and Jones out of their rooms. He unlocked Mia's door first and slowly pushed it open, seeing her pace up and down against the far wall. Once she saw the door open she stopped, wondering what was going to happen next.

"You're now free to go," Malloy told her.

"Oh. OK," Mia replied, still a bit hesitant.

"If you wait in the main office there, I'll let your friend out and then I'll take you guys wherever you'd like to go."

"Thank you," she sheepishly smiled.

As Malloy turned his attention to the other door, Mia slipped out of the room and waited in the main office. Though she had thoughts of just running out the front door as quickly as possible, it was only a fleeting thought. Jones was still in there and she couldn't just abandon him, especially after the licks he'd taken for her. As Malloy opened Jones' door, the professor was still sitting in his chair, as calm as could be. He was leaning forward with his elbows resting on his knees, and his hands clasped together.

"If you're ready we can go now," Malloy told him. "I'll take you where you need to go."

"As ready as I'll ever be," Jones replied, standing up.

Malloy held the door open as Jones walked past him. Once Jones entered the main office, Mia rushed over to him and gave him a big hug, relieved to see that he was OK, though he still had a cut on his head from the thumping that Simmons gave him. Other than that, though, he was in good shape. Jones was standing only a few inches away from where Simmons laid on the floor after his beating was administered. He looked down at the floor and noticed a small pool of blood. Knowing something must have happened, a quizzical look showed on his face. Mia noticed his strange face and looked down at the floor as well, seeing the same thing he did.

"Did something happen here?" Jones asked.

"Nothing you need to be concerned with," Malloy answered.

"It wasn't here when we came in," Mia chimed in.

"Like I said, it's nothing you need to be concerned with," he said with a smile. "Just be thankful it isn't yours."

"Whose is it?" she asked.

"I think we should probably be going. I have a car out in front," Malloy told them, ending the questions, holding his arm out to usher them along.

Mia gave Jones a look, like she was still worried about

what was to come. She still didn't feel like they were out of the woods yet. Not as long as there was a stranger, and an intimidating one at that, still hanging around. Though Vincent had kept his word up to that point, Mia still wasn't trusting of any of them. They cautiously walked out the front door, Malloy following them closely. Once they got to the car, Malloy held the back door of the car open for them to get in.

"Where can I take you?" Malloy asked.

Mia and Jones looked at each other, not exactly sure what they should say. Neither wanted to go to their house and have the man know where they lived. Although in Mia's case, it wouldn't be hard to find out, anyway. But for Jones, it was a much trickier situation. He would have to pick a completely unrelated spot or else risk giving up his role and relationship to Recker.

"Uh... if you could just drop me off at the university, that would be fine," Jones said, sticking to his cover that he just created.

Mia gave him a strange look, wondering what he was talking about. She obviously wasn't aware of the conversation he had with Vincent and had no idea about the professor identity that he was now trying to forge. Jones returned her glance and gave a slight nod with his head, trying to indicate to her to just go with whatever he was saying. He also moved his hand along the seat, trying not to be noticed by their driver, and put it on Mia's knee, tapping it a few times before putting all five of his fingers out. Although she wasn't exactly sure what he was trying to tell her, she decided she'd just roll with it. Knowing how he worked with Recker, she was confident that he had something in mind. She didn't need to know the details. She trusted him fully.

"The university?" Malloy asked. "Are you sure?"

"Yes, I know it's a little bit of a distance, but that's where I was when Ms. Hendricks met up with me this morning," Jones responded. "I'd just finished a lecture with my class and was in my office when she came over and persuaded me to join her little adventure today."

"And what about you, Ms. Hendricks? Where would you like to go?"

"Oh, you know what, might as well drop me off along with him. Like he said, I met him at the university, so my car's still there," Mia answered, playing along with the charade that Jones invented.

"If that's too far a drive, you can drop us off anywhere," Jones said. "I'm sure we can manage on our own."

"The university's fine," Malloy replied.

Malloy did as they requested and drove to Temple University, dropping the pair off near the front entrance of the campus on North Broad Street. Once Mia and Jones got out of the car, they thanked their driver for the ride and bid him adieu. As they started walking, Mia sought to clarify what Jones was doing.

"Just follow my lead," Jones stated.

"What are we doing here?"

"I told them I was a professor that taught here," he said as they walked toward the entrance.

"Why?"

"I couldn't very well tell them the truth. I can't say for

certain but I get the distinct impression that they're going to attempt to follow us wherever we go."

"Oh. Why would they do that if they're letting us go?" Mia wondered.

"To attempt to find out more about Mike. There's still a lot of mystery surrounding him. They want to know how he operates, who he associates with, who else is involved," Jones explained. "They already know you're somehow involved and I believe they highly suspect that I'm somehow involved as well. I just don't believe they know how close we are or what our roles are as of yet. But that will change rather quickly if we don't lose him and lead him back to our homes."

"So I can't go back home?"

"I think they already know about you. I believe I'm the one they're interested in."

"So what are we gonna do?" Mia asked.

"We're going to lose him."

"How?"

"Very carefully."

Once Jones and Mia entered through the front doors of the campus, Jones took a quick look back to see if Malloy was starting to follow them yet. He wasn't though, as he had yet to get out of his car. Malloy didn't want to get too near them and tip them off to his presence and make them nervous. But he knew he had to move soon. With how busy of a campus Temple was, and with several exits, it wouldn't take long to lose the pair amongst the crowd. As soon as Jones and Mia walked through the doors, they made a sharp right and continued looking at the car from a window.

"How long are we gonna wait here?" Mia asked.

"Just until he moves."

"And then what?"

"Once he comes in through the front, we're gonna slip out the side and then run across the street," Jones told her.

"Why? What's there?"

"Just a café. We can then watch a little more carefully and with some distance between us. He'll wind up searching this building for us and come up empty. Then when he finally leaves, we can go back to our own places."

Just a few seconds later, everything that Jones had said, started happening. Malloy got out of his car and started walking up to the main entrance. As soon as he did, Jones hurried Mia along, rushing over to a side door. Once they exited, they clung to the side of the building, Jones peering past the corner of the building to get a look at the entrance to see if Malloy was still there. They would have to make their move quickly. North Broad Street was an extremely busy road and if they had to stand there for a few minutes to wait for cars to go by, and Malloy happened to look through a window and see them, their plan would go for naught.

"We'll wait for a red light and then dash across," Jones said.

"Ready when you are," Mia replied.

Another thirty seconds went by before the light changed to red. With the cars stopped, Jones and Mia left the side of the building and raced across the street, just ahead of a few cars that were turning onto the street. They quickly raced up the steps into the building across from the main campus and turned into the café. It was a crowded place but Mia immediately found an open table nestled right up against the window. They instantly headed for it before the seats were snatched up, giving them an excellent view of the street and Malloy's car. Mia had a few dollars on her and got each of them a coffee while they waited. Plus, after all they'd been through, they figured they could use a boost of energy from it.

"Is this what you and Mike do all the time?" Mia asked.

"Well, not quite. At least from my perspective. Mike is usually the one in the field and having to deal with all the cloak and dagger stuff," Jones told her. "It's very rare for me to be the one doing this. I'm usually in the office doing computer work, running down leads and such. Working behind the scenes."

"How do you guys do it? I mean, it's exhausting. How do you guys not break down?"

Jones smiled at her. "It's just something that you do. Every day you learn and just try to twist every situation so that it favors you. In any case, for your doubts, you appear to be holding up well."

"I guess being an ER nurse trains you to think quickly and not get rattled," she replied. "There's no time to be nervous or scared. Otherwise, people can die rather quickly."

"This isn't that much different to be honest. Mostly quick thinking, quick reactions, knowing what you can do and what you can't. One wrong turn could be your last."

"I dunno, this is different I think. Even in the ER, you're dealing with other people's lives, but you're not dealing with your own. When Simmons had us back in that building, and even in that apartment, I really thought we were going to die. I didn't think we were ever going to make it out of there alive," she said with a sense of sadness.

"One thing about this job, profession, whatever you want to call it, you can't dwell on what almost happened, or what should've happened. In the end, all that matters is what did happen and how you learn from it, how you move on."

"Even from Mike's standpoint, I can see how it can wear a person down. Doing this all day, every day, I guess I can finally see why he is the way he is sometimes. Why he sometimes seems distant."

Jones thought about continuing the conversation and replying on Recker's behalf, but decided against it. He obviously knew that the job wasn't the only reason his partner was distant at times. But Jones didn't think it was his place to tell Mia that the other part was what happened in his previous job. Or about Carrie. That was Recker's choice to tell if he ever decided to do so. Twenty minutes had passed and Mia was beginning to wonder how much time they were going to give Malloy until they moved on.

"Do you think he knows we're here?" Mia asked.

"I think we'd have seen him by now if he did."

"What's taking him so long?"

"It's a big building," Jones answered. "I'm sure he's just being thorough."

"Maybe we should go now," Mia suggested.

"No. We'll wait for him to go first."

"What if he actually is over there waiting for us? Suppose he did see us come over here."

"Well then we'll outlast him. We'll wait him out. If he's still here in another hour or two, then we'll have to assume that he knows we're still here," Jones replied. "I really don't want to leave, though, until we see him drive away."

Malloy checked the main campus, and all the buildings and doors he could access, as well as the outside perimeter of the building in his search for Jones and Mia. He looked for an hour but they had successfully evaded his pursuit. He figured they must've slipped out somewhere but continuing to look would've been a worthless cause, he thought. They could've been just about anywhere at that point. He walked back to his car to call Vincent with the news.

"Look, there he is!" Mia excitedly yelled.

"Shh," Jones replied, reminding her they were in a public place.

Malloy sat in his car for a minute, just taking one last look around before he called his boss, hoping he wouldn't get chewed out for blowing the assignment.

"Sorry, boss. I lost them," Malloy reported.

"Where?"

"Jones told me to take them to the university."

"Main campus?" Vincent asked.

"Yeah. On Broad Street. They got out, went in the main building. I tried to follow them a few minutes later, and they were gone."

"Smart. Taking you to a busy and public place. Jones' doing no doubt."

"I should've been on them tighter than I was," Malloy sorrowfully said.

"It's OK, Jimmy. I'd still call this a successful day regardless of what happened there. Get back here so we can start preparing for Recker's arrival," Vincent told him.

"I'm on my way."

Jones and Mia looked on intently as Malloy sat in his car for a few minutes. As Vincent's lieutenant drove away, the pair started to breathe a little easier, thinking that they could finally get rid of him and find some peace after a long and trying day.

"Time to go?" Mia eagerly asked.

"Now it's time to go," Jones replied.

Mia started to get up but then quickly sat back down. "Umm, one small problem that I hadn't thought about yet."

"What's that?"

"Our cars aren't here," she told him.

"I guess we'll just have to take public transportation then."

Mia nodded before realizing the next problem they had. "OK. Uh... one more thing."

"What?"

"We don't have any money."

Jones patted down his shirt and his pants. "I left my wallet in the car before going into the apartment."

"And I just spent my last couple dollars getting us coffee," Mia said.

"I guess the only other thing we can do is... well, two things."

"Which are?"

"One, call Mike."

"He's like eight or ten hours away, isn't he?" Mia asked.

"Yes."

"And the other?"

"Beg," Jones answered.

"There's one other option," Mia told him.

"Walk?"

Mia shook her head. "No. My father's wealthy."

"Yes, I know. But I don't see how that helps us now," Jones replied.

"We don't talk to each other a whole lot. But he wouldn't leave me stranded. I'll call him and tell him to send us a cab."

"Prepaid I hope."

Mia smiled. "Relax. I got this."

Mia went up to the counter and asked to use a phone, explaining the situation to the person who worked there. Sympathetic to her problem, they handed her the phone. A few minutes later, Mia returned to the table.

"How'd you make out?" Jones wondered.

"Cab will be here in about twenty minutes. He gave them his card number and told him to charge the total to him."

"Excellent. Did he wonder what the problem was or why you were here?"

"I just told him I came up here with a friend and the car broke down so we needed a lift home," Mia answered. "Like I said, we don't talk much, we don't have much of a relationship, but he'll help me out with something if I need it. Especially if it comes to money."

"Must come in handy," Jones said.

"Eh. I suppose. I only ask favors of him if it's an emergency. Other than that, I don't really need anything from him."

"Even his love?"

"To him, sending money is showing his love," Mia replied. "That's how he shows affection."

"Well I guess in this situation, we should just be thankful for that."

10

———

Vincent had waited a little while before calling Recker to inform him of everything that had transpired. He wanted to wait until Recker got closer to Philly until he told him that he was holding Simmons at the same warehouse where they met before, the warehouse where Recker passed on the chance of evening the score with Mario Mancini. Recker didn't need to wait the additional time, though. Not since Jones and Mia had been released.

After getting picked up by the cab near the university, Mia was dropped off first, taking her straight to her apartment. Jones instructed her not to go anywhere, except for work, until she heard from either him or Recker. Just in case Vincent had someone staking out her building, Jones didn't want her to be put in danger again until they could figure out their next steps. Jones was also fearful that someone was already there watching her apartment. Just in case that was true, and someone saw them pulling up in the cab, Jones instructed his driver to drive around aimlessly for a half hour. He periodically looked back to see if anyone was tailing them, and though he never noticed anything, he didn't want to take any chances.

Jones had the cab driver drop him off at a shopping mall so he could use an ATM to withdraw some money. If someone was tailing him, not only would he lose them in the crowd at the mall, he could take a different mode of transportation out of there. Once at the machine, he patted his back pocket for his wallet, only to remember again that he didn't have it. He usually wasn't this absent minded, but the stress of the situation must have been playing tricks with his mind. With no money in hand, he walked to the other end of the mall towards the bus stop. Noticing an increasing crowd of people, Jones assumed the next stop wasn't too far away. He didn't even care where the bus was going. He'd get off wherever it stopped then call another cab to take him to his final destination, the office. After asking a couple of people, he finally found a generous woman who gave him money for bus fare. Within five minutes, the bus rolled in and Jones boarded. It's first stop was about ten minutes away, across from a gas station and convenience store, near another strip shopping center. Once he got there, the cab ride back to the office would only be another ten or fifteen minutes away.

After an hour of successfully dodging a real, or imaginary, surveillance tag, Jones finally got back to the office. He first went inside to get a credit card to pay the cabbie, then went back inside the office. He immediately sat down at his desk and went to work on the computer. Right away, he pulled up the cameras on one of the screens that he had installed six months prior to that. He had nine cameras installed, one at each end of the building near the corners, one near the entrance of the Laundromat, two near the back entrance that led up to the office, as well as two that overlooked the entire parking lot. He scrutinized the footage for the next hour, hoping he didn't see anything out of the ordinary, or any unforeseen visitors. Luckily, it appeared to be like any other night. Quiet. Once he was satisfied that there were no more signs of trouble, he grabbed one of his backup phones out of the drawer to call Recker and let him know that he and Mia were both safe. Recker's phone was on the seat between his legs, and when he heard it ring, eagerly picked it up even though he didn't recognize the number.

"Yeah?"

"Mike, it's me," Jones replied.

"Jones, you all right?"

"I'm fine. Mia's fine too."

"Where are you?"

"I'm back at the office. Mia's at home."

Recker let out a sigh of relief, finally putting his mind at ease, knowing that his friends were safe and out of danger. "Vincent released you?"

"Yes."

"I called him to see what he could do. I knew I couldn't get there in time," Recker told him.

"Understandable."

"I wonder why Vincent hasn't called me yet," Recker stated. "He said he'd call me when everything was done. How long ago did you get out of there?"

"Probably two or three hours now. I'm sure he has his reasons. He isn't one to let much go. Very thorough."

"You talk to him?"

"Yes. Quite in depth I might add, too," Jones said.

"What about?"

"Mostly questions about you. Before he released us we had an extensive interview, mostly about my knowledge of you."

"You didn't tell him anything, did you?" Recker asked.

"Of course not. I told him I was a history professor at Temple. I'm not sure he really believed that, but he didn't really press me too much on it."

"If he didn't press you then why do you think he didn't believe it?"

"Well, it was more how he asked than what he actually said. It was more like everything he said had a double meaning or a deeper meaning behind the actual question," Jones answered.

"He was probing you?"

"In a way, yes. He already knows you have a connection with Mia. There's no way around that. She had your phone number to contact you. There's no denying it. But I stuck to the story that I was just a friend of Mia's and didn't know you. I didn't have any identification on me for them to check so there was no way for them to prove otherwise unless I slipped up, which I did not," Jones explained.

"But he was still inferring that you knew me?"

"He definitely was. What do you think the meaning behind the questioning was? Mia said he did the same to her."

"He's digging for information on me," Recker replied.

"But why? It's not like you're an unknown to him anymore. I mean, you two have done several business transactions already."

"I'm still somewhat of an unknown to him. He knows what I do. He doesn't know how I do it, how I get my information, who else is working with me, who I know and associate with."

"So you think he wants to know all the fine details," Jones said.

"That's Vincent's MO. He needs information, craves it. He won't make a move for or against anything without having all the facts."

"You think he's planning something against you?" the professor wondered.

"No. Not right now at least. But what if something happens between us a year from now? He'll want to reach into his back pocket for that little black book of knowledge that he has on me. He'll want to know if he gets into a battle with me if I have anyone else with me so he can guard against all angles. If he thinks I'm a lone wolf and work alone, he only has to worry about the front door. If there are others, he's gotta guard the back door, side door, and every other entrance point you can think of," Recker explained.

"Well, I don't believe I was followed or they can trace

me in any way. Even if they find out I'm not a professor at the university, they'll have no way of finding out my identity or where we live or work. Mia's a different story though," Jones replied. "They know her name, where she works, and if they don't know already, I'm sure they'll know her address relatively soon."

"Let me worry about that."

"What are you gonna do?"

"I'm just gonna tell Vincent straight that I won't put up with any surveillance on people I know."

"We may want to rethink that strategy."

"Why?"

"If you mention anything about me or that we've talked then he will know that we are, in fact, in cahoots as they say," Jones stated.

"Well, if they start digging around the college and find out you're not working there, then they're gonna assume that, anyway."

"I suppose I could hack into Temple's system and create an additional entry with my profile and information. I'd have to create fictional courses and students to go along with it."

"Sounds like that's gonna take a lot of time," Recker noted.

"Possibly."

"Plus, isn't that something that the university will find out rather quickly?"

"Possibly."

"Seems like a lot of effort for not much payoff then."

"We'd only need it to work for a short amount of

time," Jones responded. "Just long enough for Vincent to check on my status there."

"What if he's already checked? Or what if he checks before you get that stuff into the system?"

"Then I guess I will have wasted my time."

"I don't think it's even worth the hassle," Recker told him. "If he assumes you're with me, then let him. As long as he doesn't know your real name, where you live, or where you work, it's a non-issue. Other than me, nobody else knows anything anyway."

"I suppose you're right."

"Besides, that'll take you away from other things that are more important. We need to get back to business and put this incident behind us."

"You're right," Jones agreed.

Recker continued driving, still several hours away. He wondered what Vincent was up to and why he hadn't called to deliver the news yet. In the end, it wasn't important if Jones and Mia were safe. The fact that Vincent had questioned his friends to try to find out more about their relationship to him didn't really bother Recker too much. It was something he'd expect Vincent to do at some point. It was just smart business on his part. A man in Vincent's position had to know every single detail about his friends and enemies so he could plan his next moves accordingly. As long as Vincent ended his inquisition into his friends after they were released, Recker wouldn't have a problem with it. But if he thought Mia was being followed or watched, or Jones at some point thought someone was after him, then Recker would have to lay the law down to his business acquaintance. A little after midnight, Recker's phone rang for the final time of the night. This time, it was the call he'd been waiting for all along.

"Took a while," Recker greeted.

"Yes, sorry. I hope you haven't been sweating it out all this time," Vincent replied.

"Well, I assumed since you hadn't called that all was well like you said. There were no problems?"

"Everything went down beautifully. There were no issues and your friends are now, I assume, safe and sound in their own beds."

"Thank you."

"It was my pleasure, Mike. I'm glad I could help. Just to set the record straight and before you hear it from the mouths of your friends, I just wanted to let you know that I did question them before letting them go," Vincent said.

"Question them? What about?" Recker asked, pretending like he didn't know a thing about it.

"About you. Just wondering about how they fit into your life. I hope you don't mind but I'm sure you can appreciate my position in that I need to know as much as possible about the people I do business with."

"I don't mind. In fact, I'd expect it. I could've saved you the trouble, though."

"How's that?"

"They don't. They don't fit in. First of all, I don't have friends. Can't afford to. Second, I don't know who the guy is, only that she's a friend of Mia's somehow."

"But the girl's a different story?" Vincent asked.

"She's a nurse. I figured it could be useful to know

147

someone who could help me in the case of emergencies without needing to go to a hospital," Recker answered. "I'm sure you understand that."

"I do. And it's very smart thinking on your part."

"But she doesn't mean anything to me personally. Just someone I keep around at arm's length in case."

"Must be hard to do that with someone who's as pretty as she is," Vincent assumed.

"Doesn't mean anything to me. And I thank you for your honesty in telling me all that, but it does raise one concern for me."

"What's that?"

"Since she is a contact of mine, and I'm sure you now know where she lives and works, I can't have her feel like she's being threatened, or watched, or followed in the hopes of finding out something else about me," Recker said.

"I understand your concern. And I give you my word that, as far as I'm concerned, my enquiry into their lives and how they fit into yours is over. I give you my word that they will not be watched or followed at any time. And if you ever find that they are, it is not by my doing."

"Understood."

"Good. Now that we have that out of the way, how far out of town are you?" Vincent wondered.

"About an hour or so."

"Fantastic. Why don't you head over to the warehouse where we conducted our previous business when you get in?"

"What for?"

"Oh, I've got a little surprise for you that you may be interested in."

"I'll be there," Recker agreed.

"We'll be waiting."

After Recker put the phone down, he wondered what Vincent had in mind. Considering that's where they held Mancini for him before, Recker could only assume that they had something similar in mind once again. The only problem in Recker's mind was that he wasn't looking for anybody that would lead to such a situation again. Unless it was Simmons. The longer Recker thought about it, that was the only solution that made any sense to him. It had to be Simmons. And while he hadn't given much thought to Simmons' situation after Vincent got involved, he just assumed that Vincent either killed him or sent him packing somewhere.

Somewhat surprisingly, Recker didn't feel all that much rage toward Simmons. Was the long drive cooling off his temper? Or was it the fact that both Jones and Mia wound up being unharmed? If the situation didn't go down as it did, and Simmons had his way, then Recker's anger probably would've still been off the charts. And there was no distance that would have cooled it. For the rest of the drive, Recker's thoughts stayed with Vincent and the person that he assumed he was holding at the warehouse. Though he still didn't know what Vincent's game was. If he wanted Simmons dead, he easily could've done it himself. After all, Simmons was one of his men. He wouldn't need Recker to finish him off.

The only other reasoning that ran through Recker's

mind was that it was some weird test. Did Vincent just want to see how far Recker would go to protect his friends or acquaintances? After what happened with Mancini and the fact that Recker passed up the opportunity for revenge, he wondered if Vincent was evaluating him in some form or fashion. If it turned out that Simmons was being held as a test case for Recker, he thought it might be a situation that he couldn't back down from. If things had gone down differently, and Simmons had taken Mia out of town, there was no doubt in Recker's mind that he'd hunt him down and kill him. But since things transpired differently, there was now wiggle room in Recker's mind about Simmons' ultimate fate.

If Vincent was holding his man there to see if Recker would take the bait, he thought he just might have to do it. Vincent saw him pass up the opportunity to do it once. If Recker did it twice, that might indicate weakness to the crime boss. If Recker didn't make a strong statement, he thought he might be telling everyone that it was OK to mess with people that he knew. That there would be no consequences. The longer Recker thought about it, the more convinced he became in his opinion that he'd have to swing a heavy hammer in this situation.

Whether it was real or just imagined, Recker couldn't risk a similar situation happening again. If he did nothing and let Simmons go, and word got around that The Silencer didn't retaliate for messing with his friends, then that would put Mia in even more jeopardy. Others may do the same to her or even worse without feeling at risk of Recker's wrath. Even Vincent himself may begin to think that Recker wasn't as lethal as he thought he was. Vincent might think that Recker didn't have the mean streak that most people believed he did. How he'd handle the situation, if that's what it was, was all Recker thought about for the rest of the ninety-minute drive back to Philadelphia.

Once Recker got back within the city limits, he called Vincent to let him know he was about twenty minutes away so they'd be expecting him. When Recker got to the front gates of the warehouse, he was let in without a problem or Malloy coming out to clear him. He drove up to the main building, with it looking almost exactly the same as it did the last time he was there. There was one open bay with the door open and a light on. When Recker parked, he just sat in his car for a few moments and took a deep breath, preparing himself for what he was about to walk into.

Recker got out of the car and started walking toward the side door. His legs were feeling cramped and his heart was racing as he thought about what was inside. Before he got to the steps the door opened, Malloy revealed himself within the frame of it. Malloy held the door open as Recker walked up the steps and walked inside.

"I see you guys haven't decorated much," Recker quipped.

Malloy briefly laughed before leading Recker across the floor to the side office in the back. The same one that they held Mancini in. When they got there, Malloy stopped just in front of it, letting Recker go in first. Recker instantly saw a man sitting in front of him, behind a desk and tied to a chair. Just as Mancini was before. And just like the Mancini incident, there was a gun just lying there on the desk. Recker briefly looked at him before turning his attention to the left, seeing Vincent standing there with a grin on his face.

"Hello, Mike," Vincent greeted. "Hope your drive wasn't too tiring."

"I've had worse."

"I'm sure you have."

"Who's this?" Recker asked, though he was already sure of the answer.

"That is our friend Joe Simmons."

"Looks like he's seen better days," Recker replied, noticing the numerous cuts and bruises on the man's face.

"Haven't we all?" Vincent asked, smiling.

"Why's he here?"

"Well, you see, this is an interesting predicament we've now found ourselves in."

"How so?" Recker wondered.

"The question is now what do we do with him. If we let him loose, he could always be considered a danger to you and your friends... or non-friends as they were. And for me... well, he's endangered my operations by operating outside of my guidelines that I have set forth," Vincent explained.

As they were discussing him, Simmons was wriggling around in his chair, trying to say something. It was just muffled sounds, though, as the gag in his mouth prevented anything he said from being heard clearly. Malloy wasn't pleased with his efforts though and gave him a hard slap to the side of his head to indicate his unhappiness, quieting Simmons' movements.

"I'm honestly at a crossroads in determining the best course of action here," Vincent facetiously said.

Recker wasn't fooled in the slightest. He knew exactly what Vincent wanted. Vincent wasn't the type of man who usually struggled in making a decision. He was usually swift and decisive in determining what he wanted. Just as Recker suspected as he was driving there, Vincent was testing his resolve. He wanted to see just how cold-blooded Recker could or would be.

"Are you?" Recker asked. "I think you know exactly what you want to happen here. Seems like we were in this position once before."

"Well, circumstances are somewhat diff..."

Recker didn't see the need to listen to any more of Vincent's nonsense or games. They all knew what was supposed to happen there and Recker didn't feel like putting it off any longer. He didn't even let Vincent finish his sentence as Recker quickly reached for the gun on the desk, interrupting Vincent's thoughts. Recker pointed the gun at Simmons' chest and unloaded the clip. Pop. Pop. Pop. Pop. Pop. Pop. Six shots. Only the first one was truly needed as Simmons died after the first bullet penetrated through his body. But Recker felt like making an extra statement by emptying the gun's chamber.

Vincent and Malloy just stood there looking at the lifeless body of their former employee, somewhat stunned at the quickness and decisiveness of Recker's actions. Since Recker didn't kill the man who shot him, Vincent had reservations about whether he'd pull the trigger in this instance either. He just wasn't sure if Recker was as vicious as his reputation seemed to entail. And though Vincent didn't have an exact preference for which way Recker would go, it would go a long way in determining how Vincent proceeded in the long run. Killing Simmons so quickly and ruthlessly seemed to enforce the notion that Recker wasn't a man to be messed with. If Recker hadn't, Vincent may have thought that perhaps he could take some liberties against him in the future if the need ever arose. Those thoughts, even if they were small in nature, had now been effectively squashed. Vincent had never seen Recker's work firsthand. He'd only heard second hand stories up until that point. But he was now satisfied that Recker was the man that he assumed him to be.

Recker didn't feel the need to stick around and admire his work any longer than necessary. He also didn't feel like sticking around to shoot the breeze or talk about what just happened either. He immediately nonchalantly tossed the gun to Malloy, who caught it in his midsection. Recker then just turned and looked at Vincent, giving him a nod before leaving the room.

"Thanks for the help," Recker told him.

"I'll put the bill in the mail," Vincent joked, getting a smile from his visitor.

Recker walked across the warehouse and out the side door on his way to his car. Vincent and Malloy emerged from the office and watched him through the open bay door as Recker drove away.

"That was quick," Malloy stated.

"Yes. Much quicker than I had anticipated," Vincent replied. "I expected there to be some conversation, some back-and-forth banter between us, but this worked out just as well."

"How you figure?"

"Each interaction we have with him reinforces our beliefs or strengthens our opinions in one way or another," Vincent explained. "After the Mancini incident, I must admit I had some doubts about him, even if they were fleeting. But this does reinforce what I've believed all along."

"Which is?"

"That he's not a man you want to cross. He's somewhat of a curiosity, don't you think?"

"In what way?" Malloy wondered.

"You saw how he acted against Mancini. Here was a man who tried to kill him, actually shot him, and he didn't seek revenge upon him. Even seemed indifferent towards his execution. Then there was tonight. Never met the man before, didn't do any actual harm to him whatsoever, but he acted quickly, decisively, ruthlessly. And with anger."

"So what's that say to you?"

"That you don't mess with the man's friends," Vincent answered. "He's more concerned with their safety and well-being than he is with his own. And that's a dangerous quality."

11

With having such a long day, Recker slept late the following morning, not waking up until eleven. After the killing of Simmons, Recker went straight to his apartment and went to bed. He sent Jones a short text message after leaving the warehouse telling him everything went well and that he'd see him later in the afternoon. Jones didn't bother inquiring into the events at the warehouse at that point, knowing there'd be plenty of time to go into it the next time Recker came into the office. He knew his partner must've been exhausted and wouldn't have been bothered if he even took the entire day off. Jones wondered about whether Recker finished his business in Ohio. Recker never mentioned whether he got the job done before returning. The professor would have felt bad if his trip had been cut short because of the predicament they put themselves in.

When Recker finally did wake up, he took a quick

shower before getting on with his day. He didn't bother to eat, wanting to see and talk to Mia as quickly as possible before he did anything else. He needed to make sure she was OK. While he knew from talking to Jones that she was physically safe, Recker needed to see her with his own eyes. He needed to hear it out of her voice that there were no lasting effects. Recker once again sent a message to Jones telling him he'd be in at some point but didn't know when. He called Mia's phone a couple of times but it went straight to voicemail. He knew that she usually only turned it off when she was at work so he immediately left to go to the hospital. Knowing that she usually worked either a mid-shift or later into the night, Recker decided to wait in the cafeteria for her, knowing that she'd eventually show up when she had a break.

Recker patiently sat at a table in a corner of the cafeteria, sipping on a coffee as he calmly waited for his friend to show. After two hours of waiting, he looked at the time, but he wasn't in a hurry to leave. And he wasn't leaving until he saw her. Or until he knew she was no longer there. A lot of things went through his mind as he watched people go by. The situation Mia and Jones got themselves in the day before was the most prevalent and how close he came to losing them. He also thought about how Edwards was still out there walking around, what he did to Simmons, as well as a few fleeting glimpses of Carrie's face.

In fact, he got so lost in his thoughts that he never even saw Mia come into the cafeteria. She grabbed a few things for lunch and paid at the register. Then as she was looking for a table, she caught a glimpse of Recker sitting back in the corner. He still didn't see her and she could tell that he seemed to be in another world. Although she was happy to see him, she thought it was strange that he was there and wondered what the purpose of his visit was. She approached his table and put her tray down across from him, wondering what it was going to take for him to notice her coming. Recker's trance was broken upon seeing and hearing the tray hit the table. He looked up at her and smiled, pleased she was finally there.

"Hey," Recker happily greeted.

"Is this seat taken already?"

"Nope. Been waiting for you."

"Waiting? Why?" she asked. "How long have you been here?"

"About two hours."

"Two hours?! Why didn't you just call up and tell them to page me or something?"

Recker shrugged, not wanting to make a big deal about waiting. "I didn't want to bother you. I called your phone but since you didn't answer I figured you were here."

"Oh. Sorry, I don't have a phone right now. Mine was smashed yesterday, and I didn't get a new one yet."

"I forgot."

"Besides, it's been a pretty busy day here," she replied.

"I assumed as much. That's why I figured I'd just come down and wait for you here."

"You still should've called up."

"No big deal. I didn't mind the wait."

Mia smiled at him as she began eating. "Did you eat already?"

"Nah, this is fine," Recker replied with a shake of his head, holding his coffee up. "I'm not really that hungry, anyway."

"So what are you doing here?" Mia wondered.

"Just wanted to see you."

"Aww. You're sweet. Now what's the real reason you're here?"

Recker laughed and looked away for a moment. "Honestly, I just wanted to make sure you were OK."

"Yeah, I'm fine."

"You're sure? I know what happened yesterday must've been hard for you," he told her.

"Well, I can't say that I'm eager for it to ever happen again but I'm holding up."

"Good."

Mia looked around at the tables near them and leaned forward, making sure to keep her voice down. "What if, um, what if that guy comes back or something? What if he comes looking for me again?"

"You don't ever have to worry about him again."

"Are you sure?"

Recker nodded, "positive. He's been taken care of. He'll never be an issue for you. Forget about him."

"Now, when you say he's been taken care of, what does that mean exactly?" Mia asked, hoping it didn't mean what she thought it did.

Without coming right out and saying that he killed

him, which Recker didn't want to do, he tried to think of how he could dance around the subject.

"Just means what it sounds like," Recker said. "He's gone. You don't have to worry about him. And you can rest easy, knowing that Susan's killer was brought to justice."

"By who?"

Recker and Mia's eyes locked together for a few moments. Though he didn't regret getting rid of Simmons, he was a little hesitant to come right out and tell her that he killed him. But he didn't have to. The way he was looking at her, Mia could tell that he did. If not, he would have immediately told her that someone else did. She knew that he just didn't want to admit it to her.

"Did you kill him?" she asked.

Recker sighed and looked around again as he struggled on whether he should tell her the truth. "I don't think you really need to know the particular details. Just be happy that he's gone."

Seeing that he kept avoiding the subject, Mia assumed that he just didn't want to talk about it and stopped pestering him with questions about the subject. She took a few bites of her food as she watched him rub his hands together, fidgeting around in his chair. Recker looked like he was nervous or anxious about something. She couldn't recall him ever looking like that before. Was it the questions about Simmons that he was trying to steer away from? Still, seeing him act nervous was making her a little nervous, wondering what he was doing there. Though it would've been a sweet gesture on his part to show up and just check on her well-being, it wasn't something he'd ever done before. Of course, she'd never gotten kidnapped before either.

"Is there something wrong?" Mia finally asked.

"Wrong? No, why?"

"I don't know. Just seems like you're not yourself. You seem like you're off, like you're nervous or something."

Recker shook his head. "No. I just wanted to make sure you were good."

"You could've just called for that. Why did you specifically come here?"

"Well, I got back real late last night, and I figured you were already in bed. Then when I got up, you didn't answer your phone, so I didn't want to wait until you were done work before talking to you," Recker told her.

"Are you just pumping me for information?"

"What about?"

"About what those guys did or asked."

"No, no. Only thing I'm worried about is your safety. That's it."

"You were worried about me?" she asked, never getting the feeling that he cared for her as much as she did for him.

"Of course. You weren't touched or anything were you?"

"No. I mean, Simmons slapped me in the face once or twice and grabbed my ass once, but nothing more than that."

"OK."

"It's just that...," Mia started then stopped.

"What?"

"Uh, it's nothing. Just something that the one guy said to me."

"What was it?"

"The one guy questioned me about you."

"Vincent," Recker responded.

"Yeah. I guess he wanted to see what our relationship was."

"What'd you tell him?"

"The truth. That we were just friends, and that you saved me from an abusive boyfriend once," she answered, looking sad as she played with her food.

"And?" Recker asked, concerned.

"He said something about how a man like you doesn't really have friends or anyone who's close to him."

Recker looked at her, having an idea of where she was heading. "That's sometimes true."

"And he said that it was smart of you to keep someone like me close to you," Mia said, still looking down at the table.

"And why did he say that was?"

"Cause he said that with me being a nurse that it was smart for you to keep someone like me around in case something happened to you," she explained. "Like when you were shot and came to my apartment."

Recker leaned back and put his hand on his face, running it down past his lips and chin as he thought of a reply. He could tell that she'd given it some thought, and even if she didn't believe it to be true, it at least had crept into her mind a little bit. She worried that he might have just been using her for her skills and that he didn't care about having her in his life.

"And what do you think?" Recker wondered.

Mia didn't immediately answer and just shrugged, wiping her eye as she felt a tear start to form. "I don't know. I guess sometimes I feel like that might be true. That maybe you just keep me around because you might need me sometime."

Recker knew he had to put her mind at ease right away. He reached his hand across the table and gently grabbed hers, rubbing it slightly, not letting go of it. Once she felt his hand, she looked up at him and saw him smiling warmly at her.

"The reason I keep you around is because I want you to be in my life. Not because I need you to be," Recker told her.

"Then why do you act so carefree with me? I'll call you and you won't get back to me for three or four days. I'll ask you to dinner and ninety percent of the time you say you can't make it. I feel like you intentionally keep me at a distance."

Recker, still holding her hand, looked away as he thought of the best way to say what was in his mind. It was a topic that seemed to always pop up between them every couple of months. He could always successfully dodge away from it, but he knew that at some point, he was going to have to honestly tell her what was in his heart. And he wondered if now was the time to share that viewpoint.

"I've always felt like we shared some type of... connection or a bond," Mia told him. "Like there's something there between us. But you always just shut me out and pretend that it isn't there. Or maybe there really isn't, and it's just me hoping that there is and one day a light bulb will go off over your head and you'll see it too."

Though Recker was still hesitant to come clean about everything, he could see the pain in her eyes. Tears were forming in her eyes and he didn't want to keep putting her through the agony of not knowing exactly what their relationship was.

"Fine. I'll tell you the truth," Recker stated.

"Oh boy," Mia responded, worried. She was shaking her leg up and down as her nerves were getting the better of her as she anxiously awaited what he was about to say.

"You're right. I do push you away sometimes and sometimes I keep you at a distance on purpose."

"Why?"

"There are plenty of reasons and none are close to being anything like you're thinking."

"Just tell me and put me out of my misery."

"The real reasons are because of the man I am, the life that I lead, the things that I do, things that I've done, things in my past," he told her.

"Because of what you did in the CIA?" she asked, still not fully understanding.

"Mostly."

"But that's in the past. What's that got to do with now?"

"It's got everything to do with it," Recker huffed, still struggling with how best to describe his feelings. "Look, I like everything about you. You're pretty, smart, fearless, funny, stubborn at times... there's nothing I don't like about you. And that's what frightens me sometimes. Because I could see myself falling hard for you if I let myself."

"And you don't want that?"

"It's not that I don't want it. It's that I can't have it. I can't let it. I can't have you and you can't have me."

"But why?" Mia cried. "I still don't understand."

"Because you deserve better than me. All I can do is bring you heartache."

"You won't even give it a chance. How do you know?"

"Because I tried it once before," Recker answered, figuring it was time to reveal what he'd been hiding from her for so long. "I was engaged once."

"Oh? You've never mentioned that."

"Because it's...," Recker stumbled over his words, pain clearly still evident on his face as he thought about it. "Because it's something that I'll never get over. And it's a mistake that I'll never make again."

Mia could see how torn up Recker was over recalling his past. Though she still had trouble understanding his reasoning, she cared for him too much to not try to console him over whatever it was that still haunted him.

"What happened?" she softly asked.

Recker sighed as he began to tell his story. "A few years ago I met a woman named Carrie, and we fell in love. Without getting into every detail, I wanted to leave the CIA and settle down with her. Two years ago I was in London on an assignment. It was a setup. That scar you saw on my stomach was from that night. I was shot and bleeding badly and just walking around aimlessly until I thought of Carrie, thinking she might be in danger. So I called her to warn her and tell her what happened so she could go somewhere safe."

Mia had a feeling of what he was about to say next. She felt so badly for him as he began explaining his past. They were still holding hands, though now, she was the one rubbing his hand.

"When I called her phone, a man picked up. It was another agent. And he told me he just killed her," Recker revealed, rubbing sweat off his forehead.

"I'm so sorry, Mike."

"That's the reason why I can't let myself fall for you. I can't get involved with you and let that happen again. I won't let it. I care too much about you to let that happen again."

"But just because it happened once doesn't mean it would happen again," Mia argued.

"You don't get it. If you're with me, you will always be a target. There are people out on these streets, if they knew you were special to me, that would use you as bait in order to get to me. What you experienced yesterday would be a regular occurrence. You'd get kidnapped, followed, shot at, beat up, who knows what else? Is that what you want?"

Not knowing how to respond, Mia just looked down, obviously disappointed in what she was hearing. Recker knew he was breaking her heart, but it was something that just had to be done. For her own good.

"Listen, I'm still on the CIA's radar," Recker told her. "They're still out there looking for me. They haven't stopped looking for me and they never will. And eventually I'll pop up on one of their screens and they'll be on my doorstep. I don't want them to be at yours too."

"I understand," Mia replied, disappointment flowing from her voice.

"You deserve to be happy. You deserve someone that can make you happy. I just don't think I'm that guy."

"But you won't even give it a chance."

"If you're with me, you're always gonna have to look over your shoulder. That's not a life you should lead. That's not a life anyone should lead."

"So why do you?"

"Because it's all I know. It's who I am at this point. I can never lead a normal life even if I wanted to."

"What if you left the country?" Mia asked.

"There's nowhere you can run from these people."

"How do you even know they're still looking for you? Maybe they gave up and moved on."

"Even if they had, the things I do now still prohibit a normal life for me. I have to use different identities, stay out of view of cameras, pull a hat down over my face to avoid detection, those are things you shouldn't have to go through," Recker continued. "You should be able to come home after work and have someone there waiting for you. You should be able to look into someone's eyes when you wake up in the morning. You should be able to have a family and have kids. I can't give you any of that."

"Why does this feel like a goodbye speech?"

"I don't mean it to be."

They continued their conversation for a few more minutes, though it mostly consisted of Recker telling her why a relationship between the two of them wouldn't work. Mia couldn't help but look like she'd just been stabbed in the heart. She understood his reasoning, but it didn't help to soothe the pain. It was tough for her to understand the things that Recker had been through. It was tough for anybody who had a normal life and a regular job to get what Recker was talking about. They just couldn't comprehend what the life he led was like. Mia looked at her watch and started scurrying along.

"I'm already late. I have to go," she told him.

She had about five more minutes but she couldn't take any more of the conversation. She felt like she'd been punched in the gut, stabbed in the heart, and hit by a bus all at the same time. She gathered her stuff up and put what food remained back on the tray as she started to stand up, trying hard not to look at Recker.

"I guess I'll talk to you later," Mia said.

As Recker watched her walk out of the cafeteria, he felt terrible about making her upset. He rested his elbow on the table and put his head in his hand as he rubbed his forehead.

"This is not how I thought this was gonna go," he said to himself.

12

Recker stayed in the hospital cafeteria for another hour or so after Mia left, just thinking about everything he said, replaying their conversation in his mind. He felt like it couldn't have gone any worse. He went there to make sure she was OK, worried about her, and she left in a worse shape mentally than before Recker talked to her. He thought about waiting there the rest of the day and night until Mia was done so they could continue their conversation, so he could somehow make it right with her. Recker didn't want to leave her in such a despondent mood but he also thought that there was no way around that unless he did a complete about face in regards to what she wanted.

Eventually, he thought it was better to give her some space for a while. After their talk would she want to even be around him anymore? Instead of just sitting there doing nothing, he figured it was probably time to get back to the office and see what Jones was up to. He got back in his car and drove straight to the office without stopping.

Once he got there, he sat in the parking lot in front of the Laundromat, thinking about his options. He hadn't forgotten about Edwards. Recker wondered if the time was right to go back down there immediately and finish the job or if he should wait awhile. He wasn't even gone a day before his friends got in trouble without him there. Of course, he also realized that now that Mia's problem had been solved, there was no reason any of them should get into a situation like that again. Then there was Mia. Recker still couldn't stop thinking about her. He suddenly felt like a rush of emotions were pouring over him regarding her. Was it because her life was in danger that made him feel the things he'd been trying to bury since he'd known her? He did what he promised to himself that he wouldn't do. He let his guard down. He couldn't deny to himself any longer that he did feel an attachment toward her. But he had to fight the urge to do something about it. Recker felt strongly about not acting upon it. If they pursued a relationship, and she ended up like Carrie, he couldn't live with himself knowing another love died because of him. He sat in his car for an hour before figuring he had to get moving.

Jones noticed Recker pull into the lot via the camera feeds and wondered what he was doing, just sitting there in his car. Curiosity had gotten the better of him after his friend still hadn't exited the car after half an hour. He quickly pulled up Recker's phone records to see if he was engaged in a conversation with anybody. After seeing that he wasn't, Jones was even more perplexed than he was before. He couldn't understand what Recker was doing if he wasn't on the phone.

Once Recker finally made it up the steps and into the office, he greeted Jones and sat down at a computer. Recker put his hands on the keyboard but that's as far as he got. He sat there looking at the screen without making another move. With Mia and Edwards still on his brain, his head was in a fog. He didn't know what he was doing. He just continued to sit there for a few more minutes, his hands almost frozen on the keyboard. Jones stopped typing several times as he looked to his left, seeing that his partner seemed to be in a daze. Each time Jones looked at him, he thought, now there was a man with a lot on his brain. Recker wasn't disguising well whatever was troubling him. It was clear he had a lot eating away at him. Jones pushed his chair away from the computer and turned to face his friend, hoping he could ease his troubles away a bit. The least he could do was listen. Sometimes that was as good as anything.

"I would try to say something funny but I get the sense you wouldn't see the humor," Jones said.

Recker heard him say something, but he wasn't listening closely. "What?"

"Nothing. I was just trying to lighten the mood. Can I ask what's troubling you?"

"Nothing," Recker replied in a completely unconvincing manner.

Recker started pushing some buttons on the keyboard, but he still wasn't doing anything constructive. He was just passing time. The tone of his voice told Jones every-thing. With that one word, it sounded like Recker had the weight of the world on his shoulders. Jones thought he'd just leave him alone for a while to sort out his thoughts and went back to his computer. But it was still gnawing at him. He tried to think of what could have been depressing his friend so much. Then it came to him. After everything that went down the previous day, it didn't even occur to Jones to ask what happened in Ohio. He thought that must've been it and cursed himself for even forgetting about it. Either Recker killed Edwards and didn't get the satisfaction he was hoping for or he didn't kill him and was still upset about it. Pushing himself away from the computer again, Jones sought to re engage his partner in conversation.

"Can I ask about your trip to Ohio?" Jones wondered.

"What about it?"

"Did, uh, were you able to get the closure you were hoping for?"

"I did not," Recker directly answered.

Knowing he was part of the reason why Recker's plans failed, Jones felt badly about it. He thought there was probably something different he could have done to prevent the whole Simmons situation from happening.

"I'm sorry for that," Jones stated.

"It's not your fault."

Seeing that Recker still seemed angry, and whatever trance he was in, didn't seem to be going away, Jones tried to think of something to get him right again.

"Why don't you go back down there and finish what you started?" Jones told him.

"I dunno."

"It's something you've wanted for so long. Why put it off now?"

"I don't even know if it makes a difference anymore," Recker replied.

Jones leaned back in his chair, trying to analyze his friend's behavior. It was strange. Just a day before, Recker was fired up about going down to eliminate Edwards and try to get some sense of closure about everything that happened in London. And now, a day later, he didn't even seem to care. As Jones looked at him, he figured there must have been something else in play. Something else had to be bothering him to get in a mood like this. Jones was just going to have to figure out how to pry it out of Recker's lips. Then he thought about where Recker had been since he got back to town. Perhaps it was whatever happened when he met with Vincent.

"You never told me how things went with Vincent," Jones said.

"Yes I did. I sent you a text."

"Well, all you said was everything was fine. There's not a lot of details in that."

"What else do you need to know?" Recker asked.

"How about telling me what happened?"

"He said nobody from his organization would be watching for you or Mia."

"And what about Simmons?" Jones asked.

"He's dead."

"How did that happen?"

"I killed him," Recker plainly stated, without a hint of emotion.

"Oh. I see. I suppose you did what you had to do. You did what was necessary."

"Just like always."

"Is that what's bothering you? Killing Simmons?" Jones wondered.

"No."

Jones took him at his word. He didn't think a man like Simmons losing his life would be enough to drag Recker down into the dumps like this. Not that he thought killing anyone was an easy task. He'd probably begin to worry if he thought it didn't bother Recker at least a little bit, just as it did when he killed Marco Bellomi. But Simmons was not an innocent person. He was a murderer, kidnapper, as well as a host of other criminal infractions. He didn't think that was the kind of killing that would bother Recker the most. Not believing that to be the issue, Jones turned his focus elsewhere, wondering where else Recker had been. Was it something that just happened? Being fresh in Recker's mind would cause him to still be in that kind of mood, Jones thought. Seeing as how Recker took a long time to get to the office, Jones wondered what else he was doing up to that point. Considering he had yet to bring up Mia's name or ask how she was, Jones thought that maybe it had something to do with her. He thought it strange that Recker wouldn't have at least mentioned her or asked about her, unless he'd already talked to her.

"Get enough sleep today?" Jones casually asked.

"Yep."

"What else did you do today?"

"Not much," Recker answered.

"Have you talked to Mia?"

"Yeah."

"Is she OK?" Jones asked, trying to pry a more detailed answer out of him.

"I guess so."

"That doesn't sound promising."

"She's fine," Recker told him.

"Is that where you've been all day? Talking to Mia?"

"Just a little bit."

"Damn it, Mike, will you give me something at least?" Jones asked, his voice raised.

Recker just turned his head and glared at the professor, slightly annoyed by the tone of his voice. Jones could see by the evil eye he was getting that he must have struck a nerve. Whatever conversation Recker had with Mia was what was bothering him. More than Simmons, more than Vincent, more than even Edwards. That was telling to Jones. A man that Recker had been waiting almost two years to kill was taking a backseat to what Jones guessed to be an argument with a friend. Or was the friend part the issue? Jones had always known that the two had feelings for each other, though it was more obvious on Mia's part. But he could tell that Recker did too. He just was always able to push those feelings to the side.

"You know, sometimes, you just need the ear of a good friend," Jones stated. "Sometimes it helps."

Recker looked at the professor out of the corner of his

eye as he thought about the proposition. Recker opened his mouth as if about to say something but then thought better of it and closed it. Venting about his feelings and opening up about his emotions wasn't one of his strengths. He just did that at the hospital with Mia and that didn't wind up going so well from his standpoint. But after thinking about it for another minute, Recker figured there was no harm in talking about it with Jones since he wasn't emotionally involved in it.

"I went to the hospital to talk with her," Recker blurted out.

"Oh? What about?"

"Just to see how she was."

"And I take it things spiraled in a completely different direction?" Jones asked.

"Yeah."

"How so?"

"I don't know. We just started talking about relationships. I don't even remember how it got to that point," Recker frustratingly said.

"What was said?"

"I told her why we could never be together. The truth."

"Everything?" Jones wondered.

"Yeah. Everything. About the CIA, about London, about Carrie, all of it," Recker revealed.

"Oh. That must have been difficult. For both of you."

"You have no idea."

"I assume she didn't take it well," Jones assumed.

"No, not so much."

"Doesn't seem like you took it very well either."

Recker finally took his hands off the keyboard, throwing them in the air as he tried to articulate his feelings.

"I don't know. It's weird. It's like, since I got back all I kept thinking about was whether she was safe, how she was doing. Like, all of a sudden I started thinking...," Recker said, stopping before he said what he was feeling.

"You started thinking of her as more than just a friend," Jones finished.

"Yeah," Recker nodded.

"I suppose it was only a matter of time."

"How's that?"

"These aren't new feelings for you. You've had them for her since you met her. You've just been able to bury them until now."

"But why are they starting now? Why does it seem like I'm unable to do it now? I don't understand," Recker said.

"Emotions are a fickle business," Jones replied. "Sometimes they creep up on you when you least want them to or expect it."

"Since I've been back, I haven't been able to block her out of my mind."

"I suspect that it's because of what happened yesterday."

"I dunno. These are situations that I've been in before."

"I would say that before now, her safety was never in question. And with what happened yesterday, your emotions came to the surface because you feared that you might lose her," Jones told him.

"Maybe."

"Perhaps you finally let yourself feel something for her, something you had successfully buried, because you worried that you'd lose her like you lost Carrie."

"But Carrie was different," Recker said. He rubbed his eyes as he felt them beginning to tear up, successfully blocking them from showing.

"Is it?"

"I was in love with Carrie. We had something special."

"And maybe you've finally let your emotions show for Mia because you feel like you could have something special with her too."

"I can't. We both know that."

"Do we?"

"C'mon, David. You're the one that initially told me to stay clear of her. You knew something like this could happen."

"All I know is that she has feelings for you. You clearly have feelings for her. What's the answer? I don't know. I'm not a love doctor. I really don't have an answer for you."

"She can't be more than a friend," Recker reinforced.

"Most people don't sit in the parking lot for an hour just thinking about a friend, do they?"

Recker looked at him, realizing he must've seen him pull up on the security cameras.

"Mike, what I do know is you're a torn individual," Jones said. "You've been beating yourself up for a long time over what happened to Carrie. And I think you've tormented yourself long enough. It's consumed every breath you've taken, every step you've walked, every plan you've made, every relationship you've encountered. Eventually you're going to have to make peace with that."

"I'm never going to forget what happened," Recker argued.

"I'm not talking about forgetting it."

"Then what are you saying?"

"At some point, eventually, you have to make peace with what happened."

"Peace with who? Edwards?"

"With yourself," Jones answered. "You've put the blame on yourself for what happened as long as I've known you."

"Because it was my fault."

"That's what I mean. Eventually, you have to move on. I'm not talking about forgetting, but moving on. You've beaten yourself up inside and let it eat at you for so long."

"What else am I supposed to do?" Recker asked.

"Forgive yourself."

"Easier said than done."

"Don't I know it."

"How'd we get to talking about this, anyway?" Recker wondered. "I thought we were talking about Mia."

"It's all connected, isn't it? Because you've never forgiven yourself or made peace with what happened in London, you've denied what was painfully obvious in your relationship with Mia. Now that her life was in danger, all those feelings for her that you locked away have managed to find their way out," Jones said.

"I can't let her love someone like me, can I? Living the way that I do, being on a CIA blacklist, that's no life for her. If they showed up here tomorrow looking for me, or us, we'd have to split in a second. I can't bring her into that, can I?"

"My honest opinion?"

"Of course."

"No, you can't. You and I have made conscious decisions that have led us up to this point. We understand the risks and understand what the consequences might be. Being romantically linked to you will cause her to become a hard target because of who you are."

"So you think I should just push her away for good?" Recker asked.

"I don't know if it needs to be that drastic of a change. As long as both of you know the boundaries and don't cross them, then I don't see the harm in continuing to know each other and be friends. The difficult part will be when you're near each other, not throwing caution to the wind, so to speak."

"If she even wants that."

"I guess the thing to do would be to throw the ball in her court and see what she wants to do."

13

For the rest of the day, Recker tried to put his thoughts of Mia out of his mind. He was deeply torn on her. On the one hand, he liked her and liked being around her. On the other hand, he knew that the deeper the attachment between the two of them grew, the more danger she would be exposed to. After a little while, Recker was successful in blocking out his feelings for her and was able to start working on some of the cases Jones had pulled up.

Both Recker and Jones worked separately for a few hours, but Jones felt there were still some questions that needed to be answered. Specifically, what Recker intended to do about Edwards. Jones was never one to advocate killing anyone, no matter what they'd done, but this was a special case. Just as he'd told Recker, he wasn't sure he would ever truly find peace within himself until all the loose ends of London had been successfully tied up. And as far as Jones could tell, the last remaining piece of London that haunted Recker was the fact that Edwards was still walking around.

"What do you intend to do about Edwards?" Jones finally asked.

"I dunno. Same as before I guess."

"You guess? This has been all that you've talked about since I've known you. Finding him. And now that you did, you don't seem to care."

"Well, the one time I left here, you and Mia had your lives put in danger," Recker replied. "I'm not gonna risk you guys just so I can settle a personal score."

"Mike, I think we can handle you being gone for a day."

Recker just shot a look at his partner, thinking he had to be kidding.

"OK, that was different," Jones quickly responded. "There was a situation that was being looked into at the same time as your departure. But that's over with now. There's nothing here holding you back."

"I guess you're right."

"And besides that, if you don't get him now while you know his whereabouts, you might never get as good a chance as you have right now."

"You're probably right but why are you pushing it so much? Since when did you become such an advocate for this? If I recall, you were against this," Recker told him.

"Yes, for a long time I was. But the more I've thought about it, like I told you, you need to find peace. You need closure. And until you've done this, you will never get it."

"Fine. Maybe I'll leave tonight then."

"After you've talked with Mia?" Jones guessed.

"Guess I'll need to find closure with her too."

"Well, before you do anything, let me make sure he's still there. I'd hate for you to go down there only to realize he's left for an assignment."

Jones immediately got back on his computer and started pulling up Edwards' information. He got back into the same screen he was on before which listed the latest assignments that had been handed to Edwards. He still had to go through a few backdoor channels just to make sure that his visit stayed in secret and didn't trip off any alarms. After about ten minutes, he had the information he was looking for.

"Oh dear," Jones stated, diverting his attention between the screen and looking at the calendar.

"What is it?" Recker anxiously asked, sliding his chair over.

"It appears Mr. Edwards has been handed a new assignment."

"Where?"

"Tough to say right now. He's got a new flight itinerary though."

"Where's he going?"

"JFK in New York."

"Where's he flying out of?" Recker asked.

"John Glenn Columbus International Airport."

"When?"

"9:30 tomorrow morning," Jones answered.

"I'll have to try and get him before he gets there. Too many cameras at the airport."

"I don't know if you'll be able to get there in time unless you leave right this second. Or, perhaps it'd be better to get him once he arrives in New York. It would be easier to get lost in the crowd there."

"More of a spotlight too. There's a heightened sense of something happening in New York. It's more laid back down in Ohio, smaller airport, I think that's the better play."

"You have to leave immediately then to give yourself enough time to make it," Jones told him.

Recker didn't have the luxury of thinking about it for too much longer. If he intended on killing Edwards before he left Ohio, he had to leave now. But it also presented an additional complication. It wasn't enough for Recker just to kill his target. He didn't want to just size him up through the scope of a sniper rifle and pull the trigger. It just wasn't enough for Edwards to be dead. Recker wanted to do it up close. He needed to do it up close. He wanted Edwards to know who was killing him. Recker concluded that if he couldn't look Edwards in the eyes as he was killing him, he'd rather pass on the opportunity and wait for another chance somewhere down the road. He thought that was the only way he'd get closure.

After taking just a minute to think about it, Recker decided now was the time. He didn't want to waste any more time doing the thing that had consumed his thoughts for too long. He quickly grabbed his duffel bag and went to his gun cabinet, putting a few weapons inside to take on his journey. Before leaving, he left a few last-minute instructions for his partner.

"If anything comes up, I don't care how urgent it is, you wait until I get back," Recker told him.

"And what if Mia somehow gets involved in another issue?"

"I'm pretty sure that's over with."

"Just throwing it out there," Jones said.

"I'm serious. Whatever it is, let it ride until I return. If Mia decides to play Sherlock Holmes again for some reason, you bring her back here and lock her in," Recker said, only half kidding.

"That would be interesting."

Recker raised his eyebrows and pointed at his friend. "I mean it."

Jones put his hand up to prevent the lecture from continuing. "You have my word. No secret missions, no anything until you return."

"I'll call you when I get there."

Recker rushed out the door and down the back steps of the office, scurrying to his car. To make it down to Ohio by the time Edwards' flight took off, he knew he'd have to step on the gas pedal. About three hours into his drive, his phone started ringing. Looking at the caller ID, it was Mia. He debated about whether he wanted to answer it at the moment, but then he thought that was something he'd done too often with her. Instead of tackling the issue head on, he skirted around it, hoping it'd just somehow go away so he wouldn't have to deal with it anymore. But he didn't want to do that anymore. He owed it to himself, and more importantly, he owed it to Mia to not dance around the subject of their relationship and feelings. Recker then used his hands-free device to answer the call.

"Hey," Recker greeted.

"Hey," she somberly returned the greeting. "Umm, I just got done work and just wanted to talk about a few things if you have the time."

"Uh, yeah, sure."

"You're not too busy or anything?"

"No. Just driving right now."

"Oh. Where you going?" Mia wondered.

"I'm just on my way to Ohio."

"Is that where you were going before my little mishap?"

"Yeah. With everything that went down I had to race back here and I never got to finish what I was working on," Recker answered.

"Oh. I'm sorry about that."

"You don't have to apologize."

"Yeah, I do. That's, um, kind of one of the reasons I wanted to call you. I just wanted to say I'm sorry about... everything."

"Mia, it's fine."

"No, I mean, you were right. With everything that we talked about earlier, I never really got to say what I wanted to say to you."

"Nothing else needs to be said," Recker told her.

"Yeah it does. I just wanted to say thank you," she said, wiping her eyes as her emotions started tugging at her. "I shouldn't have been doing what I was doing. You were right. I should've left it to you or waited for you. I didn't have any clue what was really going on and I should've listened to you. I was wrong."

"You wanted answers, and you weren't getting any. I understand how frustrating that is."

"That guy that set us free, you sent him there, didn't you?" Mia guessed.

"What makes you think that?"

"Because you were away and worried you couldn't get to us in time. So you protected us the only way you could. He's that crime boss that you mentioned before to me, isn't he?"

"That's Vincent, yes."

"Did you have to make some sort of deal with him?"

"Everything turned out fine. You don't have to worry about it."

"If you had to do something unethical, or that you didn't want to do because of my stupidity..."

"Mia, it's fine," Recker repeated. "Honest, I didn't have to ki... everything worked out."

"How long are you gonna be gone this time?"

"Well, as long as you and David stay out of trouble, just a day or two," Recker laughed.

"I'll do my best."

"That's all I can ask."

"OK, well, I guess have a good trip."

"Was there something else?" Recker asked, getting the feeling that she had other things on her mind.

"Well, I kind of wanted to go over what we talked

about earlier, but since you're driving and all, I guess it can wait."

"We can talk about it now if you want. It'll help me pass the time."

"Oh. OK. Well, I'm sorry if I acted like a little school girl at the hospital," Mia said.

"You didn't."

"Yeah, well, maybe. But I thought a lot about it and I'm not gonna try and force you or push you into anything you're not comfortable with. You obviously have your reasons for whatever you decide and I'll just have to deal with it. I know I'll probably never be able to fully under-stand things that have happened in your life before you met me."

"I never wanted to hurt you. I tried my best to keep you at a distance because I never wanted to have this conversation with you," Recker replied. "That's probably my fault for trying to have it both ways."

"What do you mean, both ways?"

"I wanted you close, but not too close. I wanted you in my life but I just didn't do enough to make you think things would never go further with us."

"Yeah, you did. I just ignored the signs and figured I could break you down, eventually."

"Well, you're a hard person to push away. It's not easy resisting someone like you, you know. Some guy's gonna be extremely lucky to have you. In another life, maybe it would've been me. It just can't be in this one."

"I know," she sorrowfully responded, barely audible.

"But, um... if it's too much," Recker sighed. "If it's too

much or too hard to continue seeing me or anything and you wanna take a break or something, then, uh, I'll understand."

"Umm, I dunno, uh, let's just see how it goes."

"So I guess we're good then?"

"Yeah. Yeah, we are. We're good," Mia said. "So maybe we'll talk again when you get back."

"Sounds like a plan."

Once the conversation ended, Recker just tossed his hand-free device on the passenger seat, clearly annoyed. He started talking to himself out loud.

"When it came to handing out the good things in life, I clearly drew the short straw. Someone up there decided I wasn't worthy of having anything good in my life for too long."

Recker allowed himself to get caught up in self pity for a little while as he continued his trek to Ohio. He never was one to get lost in regrets or what-ifs or wonder what might have been if things had gone down differently in his life. Mostly because he was basically a realist at heart. He knew that sometimes, people just got dealt a harder set of cards to deal with in life and there was no rhyme or reason to it. That's just the way it was. He never wondered before what his life would be like if he never joined the CIA or enrolled into the black ops program. But after thinking about what he lost with Carrie, and what he'd never get to have with Mia, for the first time, he started thinking about what his life would've been like if he was someone else.

Of course, he knew that by doing so, he likely never

would've even met Carrie or Mia if he never joined the CIA. Everything he had done in his life had a direct impact on meeting the both of them. If he hadn't, the loss he felt with Carrie would never have been burned into his memory. And Mia wouldn't be the situation that it was. But he allowed himself to envision what life could've been like if he'd have met each of those women under different circumstances, if he wasn't the man that he was. With Carrie, he could picture himself as a family man. He saw himself coming home from work and having her there with a couple of kids running around the house. When his thoughts turned to Mia, he pictured the two of them just doing couple things, going on dates and having romantic dinners. There was a small piece of him, just for a few minutes, who wished he was someone else.

After allowing himself to dream for an hour or two about what might have or could have been, Recker finally shook free of those thoughts. It was nice while it lasted though and made the drive seem that much quicker. With those tempting thoughts now out of his system, he turned his attention back to his target. He started to envision different scenarios on how his altercation with Edwards would go down.

Recker made great time in getting back into the state, much quicker than he did the first time around. It only took him a little under thirteen hours to get there this time. As he made his way toward the Edwards home, he was a little concerned that he wasn't going to arrive before his target left for the airport. Since it was past 7am, he called Jones to see if he could help in locating him to save time.

"David, just got here, are you able to verify if he's still at home or if he left yet?" Recker wondered.

"Well, I could, but not in the timeframe that you need. It's gonna take longer than you have time for. You might be better off just heading to the airport and waiting for him there."

Recker sighed, not getting the answer that he wanted. "I was hoping it wouldn't come to that."

"Are you going to back off?"

"No. I'll make it work."

"OK. I'll do my best to start checking the airport cameras and see if I can locate whether he's there yet."

"All right. I'll put the comm in. Let me know."

Recker headed straight for the airport, hoping he'd get there before Edwards did. Once his subject checked in, and he was surrounded by a bunch of people, killing him might not be an option. And he was too close now to have to put it off one more time. Seeing that it was just a couple minutes before 7:30, and most people checked in about two hours before their flight, Recker thought he might've made it just in time. Before getting out of the car, he put on a blank baseball type hat, cinching it down near his eyes. He swiftly walked into the airport and immediately grabbed a newspaper in case he needed to use it as cover.

"Michael, it doesn't appear that he's there yet," Jones said.

Recker buried his head into his arm, pretending he

was wiping his face to conceal him talking. "Are you sure?"

"Well, all I needed to scan was the entrance cameras. I was able to hack into them rather quickly."

"How far back did you check?"

"I went back to 6am," Jones answered. "I didn't see anyone that looked like him come in yet."

"That means he should be here any minute."

"In theory."

"What, you think he might not show?"

"I don't know. Until it happens it's never a sure thing, is it?"

Recker found a wall to lean against as he anxiously awaited for his foe to arrive. He opened up the paper to pretend he was reading it, instead peering over the top of it as he watched people enter through the front doors. After ten minutes went by, he started to get a little nervous that his target was even coming. Had Edwards got last-minute orders to change flights or not even go at all? He figured he'd wait another hour for him then he'd drive back out to his house and see if he was still there. If he wasn't in either spot, then Recker would have to regroup and come up with another plan. He was praying that it wouldn't come to that though. He was ready for it to be over now.

Luckily for Recker, if he did say a prayer, it was answered. His attention perked up at 7:50 when he saw Edwards strutting through the door. With a small bag that he was wheeling behind him, he had a confident look and walk about him, like he had no worries in the world. That was about to change if Recker had his way. He briefly replayed their conversation in his mind one more time as he watched him walk by. Recker tugged his hat down even further to prevent him from being recognized. Edwards had an arrogant look on his face in Recker's mind. Of course, that could've just been because he hated the guy.

"Jones, he's here," Recker told him. "I'll contact you when it's over."

"Please be careful," Jones responded.

Recker started following his target as he watched Edwards stop at the Starbucks. Keeping his head down to conceal his face, he took up a new position as he kept close tabs on Edwards. After his target got his coffee, he started on the move again. Before heading to the gate, Edwards made his way to the bathroom as he made a last-minute stop. Sensing that it was the best opportunity that he was going to get, Recker also made a beeline for the restroom. He cautiously opened the door, just in case Edwards had spotted him and was trying to lure him in to turn the tables on him. Luckily for Recker, he hadn't.

Edwards was at the urinal, coffee still in hand, with his back turned to the door. Recker easily could've shot him and be done with it, but it just wasn't good enough. Recker quickly knelt and looked underneath the stalls to see if anyone else was there. Seeing that they were alone, Recker walked back to the door and quietly locked it. He went over to the sink and turned the water on, pretending to wash his hands. After a minute, Edwards had finished his business and walked over to the sink. He set his coffee down on the side of the sink, not having any clue as to the identity of the man standing next to him. He turned the water on and started washing his hands, giving Recker the opportunity he was waiting for.

Recker quickly turned toward his target and put his hand on the coffee, feeling how hot it was and flipping the lid off, all within a second or two. He threw the hot coffee directly into Edwards' face, temporarily stunning him as he dabbed at his eyes. Recker grabbed the back of Edwards' head and forcefully slammed it into the sink, knocking Edwards to the ground. A big welt immediately started showing on Edwards' forehead as Recker gave him a hard kick to the face, bloodying the man's nose. Recker then picked him up and threw him into the stall door, Edwards bursting through it as his head hit the bottom of the toilet. Edwards was dazed and confused and already in a lot of pain, unable to recognize who his attacker was. Recker gave his victim another stomp to the face, making sure he couldn't get up before he unleashed some more punishment. He then straddled Edwards' body and started raining down punches in a furious manner. Alternating between his left and right hands, Recker's knuckles quickly became bloodied as he opened up cuts on Edwards' face.

After a couple of minutes, Recker stopped, taking a few moments to calm himself so Edwards could finally see who his assailant was. With cuts above both of his eyes, nose, forehead, and lip, Edwards could barely open his eyes wide enough to see out of them. But Recker tried to make it easier for him, taking off his baseball hat and tossing it on the ground. Edwards tried to make a smile and let out as much of a laugh as he could, though it caused him to start coughing up some blood. Recognizing Recker immediately, he knew he was done for. Edwards stumbled his way through a few words before his time was up.

"I knew we'd have this day at some point," Edwards said, coughing. "Didn't figure it'd go down quite like this though."

"Funny how things look from different perspectives," Recker replied. "Cause this is how I always thought it would go."

"Don't suppose begging would help?"

"Nope."

Edwards smiled again, hoping to torment his attacker one last time. "You know, thinking back, I so enjoyed killing her."

That was enough for Recker. He didn't want to hear anymore. He took out his gun from the back of his pants and pointed it at his soon to be victim. Before pulling the trigger, he had some final words of his own.

"You know, talking about different perspectives, it's funny how things work out," Recker told him. "I could've done this yesterday at your house in front of your wife and son."

Recker had almost an evil smile attached to his lips as he saw the worried look on Edwards' face. He now realized that Recker knew where he and his family lived and worried for their safety. He worried that Recker would do to his family what Edwards initiated with him.

"Please, not them," Edwards pleaded.

Recker let out a laugh and pulled the trigger of his gun, hitting the front of Edwards' thigh with his shot. Edwards screamed out in anger, wondering what Recker was waiting for in finishing him off.

"Torment me all you want, just don't kill them. I beg you," Edwards pleaded again.

"I'm not like you," Recker responded. "I don't enjoy killing. Not even you."

Recker then fired three more shots in succession, all hitting his fallen target square in his chest, instantly snuffing out whatever life remained in his helpless body. He remained standing over the dead body for another minute, just staring at the carnage that he'd just unleashed upon him. With it now over with, Recker knew he couldn't stay there any longer. Sooner or later, someone else would try coming in, and with the door locked, might inquire to someone who worked there why it wasn't open. Recker looked down and grabbed his hat, pulling it back down over his eyes as he tucked his gun away in his pants again. He exited the restroom, standing on the outside of the door for a few moments to make sure nobody else entered already. He needed to make sure he had enough time to get away. After thirty seconds elapsed without anyone coming near it, Recker quickly hurried away toward the entrance. With his hat securely pulled down near his eyes, he kept his head looking toward the floor to prevent the cameras from getting a good shot of his face.

Recker got to his car and quickly peeled out of the parking lot. He periodically checked his rearview mirror to make sure that nobody was following him. Once he was on the road for about thirty minutes, he began feeling more secure in his escape. It seemed like a clean kill without any complications that would arise from it. He had forgotten to contact Jones to let him know, so he figured he would call him so he wouldn't begin to worry.

"It's done," Recker confirmed.

"I figured as much. I kept looking at the surveillance cameras and noticed you leaving a half hour ago."

"You could make me out?"

"Well, I could just because I knew the hat," Jones answered. "But you did a good job of not letting your face show so they shouldn't be able to match it back to you."

"That's good."

"I also checked parking lot cameras just to be sure they couldn't get a shot of your license plate."

"And?" Recker wondered.

"Nothing. You're in the clear. Even if it was, I could digitally alter it."

"How could you do that?"

"Did you never wonder about when you first arrived in Philly?"

"No. What do you mean?"

"Your face was picked up by airport security cameras when we had our first talk," Jones informed him. "I had to alter and erase some of the footage so it seemed as if you were never there."

"Why? You told me you did something with the flight manifest or something."

"Just in case someone went looking at nearby airports

on a hunch. They obviously knew you were on a plane somewhere. So in case they looked into every airport security system on the east coast, I had to doctor the footage."

"Oh. You never mentioned that before."

"I never thought it needed mentioning before."

"Oh. Thanks for everything."

"You're welcome."

"How's everything there?"

"Just fine. Ready to get back into the swing of things."

14

Almost the entire ride home, Recker thought about the confrontation he'd just had with Edwards. It was something he'd thought about every day for almost two years. He thought about different ways he would kill him, one of which was brutally beating him just the way he'd done it at the airport. He hoped that once it was over, a sense of relief would be lifted off his shoulders, or a bright light would suddenly shine down from the sky upon him. But it didn't happen. At least not yet. Though he did feel a small sense of satisfaction, he didn't feel anywhere near as good as he hoped he would. He was obviously glad that he found Edwards and eliminated him, but it would never bring Carrie back. What Recker lost that night in London would never return to him, no matter how many revenge killings he had. Everything was still fresh in his mind, though, and maybe in a few days or weeks, things might look much different to him. He could only hope that Jones was right in that doing this would bring the closure he needed to keep going. Hopefully, he just needed more time to get to that point.

Recker took a little extra time on the way back than he did getting down to Ohio. He didn't see the need in driving faster and risk getting stopped by the state police somewhere on the road. He finally got back to the Philadelphia area around one in the morning and went straight to his apartment to try to get some sleep. There was nothing so pressing on Jones' list of potential victims that couldn't be started the next day. After an action-packed couple of days without getting much of a chance to rest, Recker fell asleep within minutes of his head hitting the pillow.

Getting back to the office the next day around ten, Recker brought a couple of breakfast sandwiches with him. Jones was already there, hard at work as usual. The professor had his list of targets that they needed to work on and he was putting on the finishing touches to his reports, checking out some background information on the first couple of people. He took a brief break, however, when Recker handed him his food and the two men began eating at the desk.

"Just so you know, your airport situation is all over the news," Jones said.

"Figured it would be. Airport killing is a big deal."

"Yes, it is. Regardless, I'm trying to keep ahead of the situation and monitoring it to see what kind of leads they come up with."

"Anything yet?" Recker asked.

"No, not so far. You did a good job in disguising your-self so I don't expect any repercussions."

"What are they saying so far?" Recker wondered. "What are they saying he is? International hit man?"

"Hardly. They're saying he's a security consultant who had clients with ties to organized crime."

"About what I figured."

"Well, I'll keep monitoring it in any case. You certainly look a little more refreshed though," Jones told him.

"Yeah, I feel a little better."

"It's amazing what a few hours of sleep will do for you."

"Yeah," Recker replied, though still not looking pleased.

"So what's wrong?" Jones asked, sure that something still seemed to be bothering him.

"I dunno. It's just that... I don't feel all that much different than I did a few days ago."

"You mean before killing Edwards?"

"Yeah."

"Well what did you expect?" Jones wondered.

"I don't know," Recker shrugged. "I just thought maybe I'd feel... happier or something."

"Mike, you've felt a certain way for a very long time. That's been ingrained into your soul and well-being with every step you've taken. The darkness that's been milling around inside of you isn't just going to evaporate overnight. It will take time."

"Yeah, I guess."

"Believe me, it will happen. Little by little, you'll get to a better place. Eventually your mind will get to a clearer place. But it will take time. You just have to be patient with it."

"OK. I, um, talked to Mia again last night," Recker revealed.

"Oh? How did that go?"

"I guess we'll see. She wanted to apologize and thank me for the other day."

"So she isn't upset now?"

"Well I don't know about that. She seemed more understanding of my position I guess."

"What else did you say?" Jones wondered.

"I told her if what we have now is too hard for her then I'd understand if she didn't want to come in contact anymore."

"Oh. What did she say to that?"

"She said we'll see," Recker answered.

"And what do you think she'll do?"

"I really don't know."

"And what are you hoping?"

Recker just shook his head. "I really don't know that either. I just want her to be happy. And I know that won't include me."

The pair finished their conversation over breakfast and got back to work. They started analyzing each of the cases on their list and started coming up with a game plan on how to act with each of them. They only got about thirty minutes into their work when they were interrupted by the sound of Recker's phone ringing. Recker looked at the ID and was a little perplexed at the caller.

He couldn't figure out what purpose they'd have for calling him now.

"Miss me already?" Recker sarcastically asked.

Malloy laughed, appreciating his sense of humor. "No, not quite. Boss wanted to talk to you. Here he is."

"Mike, how are you?" Vincent greeted.

"All right. Kind of surprised to be hearing from you to be honest."

"We've had a good relationship so far and I want to keep up the bond that we're developing."

"Sounds like you're about to drop some bad news on me," Recker guessed.

"Possibly. I'll get right to it then. Based on what transpired the other day, I've heard some rumblings that something may be going on that I wanted to alert you about."

"Which is?"

"Joe Simmons has a cousin who's apparently none too happy about his death. From what I hear, he's sworn to avenge the people that were responsible for it," Vincent revealed.

"So why don't you put a stop to it?"

"He doesn't work for me. I don't really know much about him. I don't have a file on him or anything. Like I said, he's not a part of my organization. All I know is he lives in Jersey."

"Then how do you know about him?" Recker asked.

"I have a lot of eyes and ears on the street. One of my contacts informed me that he heard about his unhappiness."

"So who's he gunning for? You or me?"

"Well, from what I understand he doesn't know of my involvement in the situation. How that is, I don't know," Vincent answered.

"So that leaves me."

"There's more."

"Go ahead."

"I've heard he's also going after your nurse friend."

"Mia?"

"From what I understand, he holds her chiefly responsible," Vincent said.

"How's he even know about all this?"

"That I don't have an answer to."

"What's this guy's name?" Recker asked.

"Jason Gallagher."

"Thanks. I appreciate you looking out."

"If you need anything else just ask," Vincent told him.

As soon as Recker put the phone down on the desk, Jones could tell that he was deeply troubled by something. Hearing Mia's name in the conversation, he had a feeling it had something to do with her, but he couldn't figure out what. Not yet. Recker stood and put both of his hands on the edge of the desk as he leaned forward, looking down as he took a deep sigh.

"What is it?" Jones hesitantly asked with great concern.

"Simmons apparently has a cousin who wants revenge for what happened to him."

"Vincent?"

"He doesn't work for Vincent," Recker replied. "He

doesn't know much about the guy other than he lives in Jersey."

"How does this guy know it was you involved?"

Recker shook his head in frustration for having to deal with another problem. "I don't know."

"Is he after Vincent as well?" Jones wondered.

"No. He doesn't know about Vincent's role in it."

"That's strange."

The two men stayed silent for another minute as they deliberated on what to do next. They obviously would have to protect Mia while at the same time finding Gallagher before he had a chance to enact his plan of revenge. Then Jones made a sound and looked at Recker as if an idea just popped into his head.

"What is it?" Recker asked.

"What if Simmons called this guy before everything went down, before we met him and told him that Mia was looking for him?" Jones wondered.

"Could be."

"Or, perhaps even after Simmons took us, before Vincent arrived, maybe he called his cousin to tell him what happened?"

"Could be."

"Let me dig into Simmons' phone records and see if he placed any calls."

"Might as well check into Jason Gallagher from Jersey while you're at it."

"We should've done this before as a precaution," Jones huffed. "Just to be sure there'd be no repercussions. I don't know why we didn't."

Jones feverishly typed away, trying to get into Simmons' phone records. After a few minutes, he successfully hacked into them. He looked down the list of numbers that Simmons called and saw that he placed a call at 1:15pm, a little over an hour after the supposed meeting with Jones and Mia that resulted in their capture. Armed with that knowledge, Jones typed in Jason Gallagher's name into their database, quickly getting a hit on his name. Jones also typed in the number that Simmons called, and it came back as belonging to Jason Gallagher.

"There's the connection," Jones noted.

"After Simmons took you guys, he called Gallagher and told him what was going on," Recker assumed.

"What do you want to do now?"

"I'll go to Jersey and pay this guy a visit."

"Maybe we should call Mia and let her know to be careful," Jones said.

"I don't want to worry her if we don't have to."

"Well I don't want you traveling to New Jersey only to find out he isn't there. What if he's already on the move? Let me try pinging his cell phone."

After a couple minutes and a few shakes of Jones' head, Recker could tell that he wasn't having much luck in his endeavor.

"I'm gonna go," Recker insisted.

"Just wait," Jones replied. "Let me try a couple other things."

"Such as?"

"I can hack into the GPS on his phone if it's been enabled recently and pull up his position that way."

About five minutes passed and Jones made a few gestures to his partner indicating that it was working out.

"I got it," Jones stated.

"Great. Where is he?"

"Not in Jersey. He's on the move."

"Where?"

Jones stopped typing and turned to look at Recker. "Here."

"Here? Where? The parking lot?" Recker asked.

"Not here. Here. Philadelphia."

Recker, fearing what was about to come out of Jones' mouth next, clenched his jaws. "Where is he now?"

"I think he's heading for the hospital."

"How much time do we have?"

"None," Jones puffed. "It looks like he'll be there any minute."

Recker immediately grabbed his phone and dialed Mia's number, desperately hoping that she'd pick up. It rang several times but just went to voicemail.

"Check if she's working," Recker told his partner.

Within a couple minutes, Jones easily hacked into the hospital time management system. It was a process he'd done several times before so it wasn't much of a challenge to him since he was already familiar with it. She was scheduled to work at eleven, though she hadn't yet clocked in.

"She's not picking up," Recker worriedly said.

"I think I made a mistake."

"What?"

"I'm looking at the time stamps and locations of Gallagher's phone," Jones replied.

"What's wrong?"

"I don't think Gallagher's on his way to the hospital."

"Then where is he?" Recker asked.

Jones looked at Recker, almost afraid to deliver the news. "I think he's already been there."

"Why do you say that?"

"The time stamp on the GPS on his phone indicates he was at the hospital's coordinates at 10:45," Jones answered. "The next one at 10:55 indicates he's moving away from there."

"He was there waiting for her," Recker assumed.

"I'm afraid it looks that way. She was supposed to work at eleven. It's now 11:30, and she hasn't clocked in yet."

Recker got a maniacal look in his eyes, like he was about to rip someone's head off. Though he wasn't mad at Jones, Recker stared at him for a minute as he let the anger flow through his veins.

"How could we be so stupid?" Jones angrily asked, slapping at his keyboard out of frustration.

Recker took control of his anger, not letting it get the best of him yet, and started to think clearly about the best way to proceed.

"That hospital has security cameras," Recker stated.

"I'm on it," Jones quickly replied.

Recker took a seat again, rolling it over next to Jones as they got into the security footage. Jones rolled the cameras back to 10:30 and fast forwarded a little at a time as they looked for Mia somewhere on the screen. At 10:50, Jones paused the screen, clearly seeing Mia get out of her car after she parked in the lot. They slowly played the footage, outraged at seeing three men quickly approach her only moments after exiting her vehicle.

"What's that there?" Recker asked, pointing to something on the screen. "In that guy's hand near her back."

Jones quickly zoomed in on the object, not liking what he saw. "It's a gun."

"Can you get into her phone and see where she's at?"

Recker leaned forward and put his head in both of his hands as he rubbed his face. His mind was racing with horrible thoughts that Mia was already dead. If he lost her too, there was no telling what type of destruction was about to commence. Jones looked over at his friend and could tell he was in a considerable amount of mental anguish as he thought about Mia's fate. The news he had to tell him wasn't going to make it any better.

"I locked into her phone's GPS system as well," Jones told him.

"And?"

"It's still at the hospital."

Recker started rocking back and forth in his chair, feeling like he was about to go full bore psycho on someone. Seeking to calm his friend, Jones offered up a few solutions to quell his rage.

"If they wanted her dead yet, they probably would've done it already," Jones told him. "If they were going to kill her, they wouldn't have taken her with them."

Recker stopped rocking and looked at Jones. "They need her for something."

"Maybe Simmons told her there was a man with her. Maybe they're looking for me."

"Or Simmons told him that she was a link to me," Recker replied. "Either way, I'm the one they're getting."

"Before this gets out of hand any further, we have a valuable asset on our side," Jones said.

"I don't know if we need to get Vincent on this."

"No. I don't mean him. I mean we already have Gallagher's phone number."

"I'll call him and see what he wants," Recker said.

Recker picked up his phone and looked at the screen to see Gallagher's number. He dialed the numbers, but waited a second before hitting the call button. Recker then hit the button and anxiously waited for Gallagher to pick up. It went to voicemail though.

"Maybe he's one of those people who don't answer numbers they don't know," Recker wondered. "I'll send him a text."

"Pick up the phone idiot," Recker texted.

Almost immediately, he got a text back. "Who this?"

"Pick up and find out."

Recker's phone rang almost instantly, this time, Gallagher calling him.

"Yo, who the hell are you?" Gallagher asked.

"I hear you might be looking for me," Recker answered.

"I'm looking for a lot of people."

"That girl you just took from the hospital better be unharmed."

"How'd you know about that?"

"Doesn't matter. What does matter is what you do from here," Recker angrily told him.

"What's your interest in this?"

"Cause I'm the one that killed your cousin," Recker revealed.

"You dirty rotten son of a bitch. I'm gonna kill your..," Gallagher started to threaten.

"Enough threats. The girl has no stake in this. I'm the one that killed your cousin. You got a problem with that, then take it up with me."

"Oh, I intend to."

"Let her go and give me a time and place and I'll be there."

"Or maybe I'll just kill her right now, then come for you."

"I wouldn't do that," Recker told him, looking at the computer screen for his personal information.

"Why not?"

"Cause I see that you live in Cherry Hill. That's not too far from where I am right now. In fact, I could probably make it there before you do. You probably wouldn't want to go back there anyway, mom might not wind up looking so good," Recker warned.

Gallagher was speechless for a second, knowing that the man knew where he lived. "How do you know that?"

"Doesn't matter. What does matter is if you harm that

woman with you, I will visit your home and kill every single member of your family and I'll do it without hesitation. You want retaliation for your cousin, then take it up with me."

"Fine. One hour. Mercer Cemetery in Trenton. Come alone or else I'll kill her on the spot."

Jones quickly googled Mercer Cemetery to get a look at the layout of the area. They studied it for a few minutes before Recker decided to go.

"If I leave right now, I might be able to get there before they do," Recker said. "We're closer to Trenton than the hospital is. Those idiots shouldn't have told me a spot to meet until they got there."

"I'm assuming they didn't realize you knew their exact location," Jones replied.

"Their mistake."

"I'll keep on tracking their GPS signal but there is one other problem."

"What's that?"

"What if they meet you in the cemetery but keep Mia in the car with a guard to make sure there's no problems? If you kill the others, maybe they'll kill her regardless," Jones mentioned.

It was a situation that Recker hadn't thought of, but it certainly seemed plausible. He'd need another person with him in that event.

"I guess you're volunteering," Recker told him. "Can you still track him remotely?"

"Of course I can. Who do you think you're talking to?" Jones responded, quickly grabbing a laptop.

Recker hurried out the door once more as he seemed

to do all too often the last few days. Though he had the advantage of knowing the meeting spot, he was at a disadvantage of not knowing how many men Gallagher had with him. If it was whoever could fit into one car, knowing they had Mia, he probably had no more than three or four men with him. Recker raced down route one until he got into New Jersey. They got to the cemetery in about twenty-five minutes and pulled up to the curb just down the street from it.

"There's bound to be witnesses here," Jones noted. "Too many people not to be. Plus, there's offices right across the street."

"Can't worry about that right now."

"I know. I'm just saying."

"Nobody's there yet. Looks like we beat them there," Recker said.

Recker reached toward the floor of the back seat and unzipped his duffel bag, pulling out several guns. He kept three for himself and handed one to Jones.

"You may have to use this," Recker told him, handing him the weapon.

"I know."

"You can't hesitate or we all might wind up dead."

"I'll do what has to be done," Jones confidently stated.

"I'm gonna go to the back of the cemetery and wait for them. Let me know when you first put eyes on them."

Even though Recker initially thought about going to the back and waiting, he saw a big statue near the front, easily capable of hiding him from Gallagher's view. They waited another twenty minutes, anxiously looking out for their intended victims. As Gallagher's car pulled up, Jones got out and walked to the corner of the cemetery, waiting by the brick siding. Gallagher and three men got out of the black SUV, looking like they were in a hurry. Mia did not get out with them. Jones could only assume that she was still in the car.

"Mike, they're here," Jones told him.

"Mia?"

"I don't see her."

"Check the car," Recker replied. "How many are there?"

"Four walking in now."

"This is gonna happen quick. Check the car now."

Jones scurried over to the car, but did so in a way where it didn't appear he was running right for it. He looked through the back window but couldn't see much through the dark-tinted glass. He cautiously walked around to the back window on the passenger side and peered through, still not seeing anything. Knowing he had to get in there somehow and was running out of time, he forcefully knocked on the glass. If someone was there, he figured he'd just pretend to ask for directions. He got no response though. Jones knocked once more but still heard nothing. He tried to open the doors, but they were locked.

"Mia?" Jones shouted.

He put his ear up to the window as the car started shaking slightly. Jones took a step back and looked at the car. Someone was moving in there.

"Mia, are you in there?" Jones asked again.

He put his ear up to the window again and thought he

heard some muffled screams, though they were faint. Figuring they left Mia alone but tied up, Jones took a quick look around to make sure nobody saw what he was about to do. With the coast clear for the time being, Jones took the handle of the gun and smashed the driver side window open. He reached his hand in and unlocked the door, getting in the seat and quickly taking a look toward the back. There was Mia. She was on the floor of the back seat, tied up and gagged but otherwise unharmed. Jones reached back and took the gag out of her mouth.

"Are you OK?" Jones asked.

She was breathing heavily from the scare she'd gotten, but was relieved to see the professor. "Yeah, I think so."

Jones unlocked all the doors, then got out and opened the back door to help Mia get out of the car. He untied her ropes and helped her out of the car. Thrilled to see him, Mia gave him a hug so hard that it almost squeezed the life out of him.

"I'm so happy to see you," Mia said.

"We have to go to the car," Jones replied.

"Is Mike here?"

"Yes, and we're going to have to move very quickly in a minute."

"Why, what's going on?"

"You're about to hear it in a minute."

Jones took Mia by the hand and the two of them ran back toward his car. He knew they'd have to get out of there fast once the shooting started. To avoid any police entanglements, Recker would most likely be running toward the car as quickly as possible. Mia tried looking back toward the cemetery to see if she could see Recker but they were moving too quickly for her to find him.

Recker was still standing behind the ten foot high statue, out of sight from Gallagher and his men. He patiently waited there, looking to both sides of him, ready to start firing in each direction. He stuck his ear out, hoping to catch them talking or even moving closer to him.

"Where's he at?" one of the men asked.

"Spread out," Gallagher stated.

They were hoping that once they found Recker they could surround him or at least trap him, with two of them meeting him head on and the other two coming up on each side of him, leaving him nowhere to go. Recker knew one was about to come up behind him on his right and readied to fire. He moved a little closer to the corner edge of the statue as he readied to pounce on the unsuspecting man. He quietly listened for the man to step on a twig or a leaf, giving his position away.

Once he did, though, Recker knew he'd quickly have to locate the others as then bullets would start flying fast and furious in every direction. Ten seconds later, Recker heard a leaf crunching underneath a heavy foot. Giving the man a few more seconds to pass his position, Recker stepped away from the statue as he had the man in his sights. Recker calmly put his gun up to the back of the man's head and put a hole through it.

"What was that?" Gallagher worriedly asked, turning to the direction of the shot.

Almost immediately after firing the shot, Recker

jumped back behind the cover of the statue, waiting for the others to come running. If he was lucky, he could gun them down rapid fire. Gallagher and the man he was with slowly started walking over, unsure what they were walking into. Knowing they were relatively close, Recker figured he could get the jump on them and surprise them. He emerged from the shadow of the statue, catching the two hoodlums completely off guard. As soon as Recker saw the outlines of the two men, he fired six shots at them in succession, not even giving them a chance to return fire. Four shots wound up hitting Gallagher, the other two hitting his friend. Both men died instantaneously.

As Recker looked at the two dead bodies in front of him, another shot rang out from the remaining crew member. The shot whizzed past Recker's head, grazing off the statue behind him. Recker dropped to a knee and quickly identified where the shot came from and located his target. Dodging another bullet in his direction, Recker returned fire with a couple shots of his own. His missed as well. Figuring he couldn't stand there all day in a shootout and wait for police to arrive, Recker took matters into his own hands. He stood and calmly started walking toward the man.

With bullets flying past him, Recker didn't even flinch. He looked and acted like he had a suit of armor on that the bullets couldn't penetrate. But just like that night in London, he believed that he was just as likely to run into a bullet as it was if he took his time. He also knew it wasn't normal behavior and thought it might intimidate whoever was firing on him, causing them to panic knowing that he was coming closer, making their aim worse as they fidgeted around with their weapon. As Recker closed in on his target, the man eventually ran out of bullets. He kept firing, though, hoping somehow a bullet would magically emerge from the chamber. Once Recker had him in his sights, he saw the worried look on the young man's face, thinking his life was soon to be over. And he was right as Recker quickly put the man out of his misery and fired two shots that hit him in the chest.

"David, pull the car down the alley," Recker told him, looking at all the dead bodies.

There was a seldom used alley to the side that led around to the back of the cemetery that Recker figured would be an easier escape path. If he just walked out the front, there were sure to be prying eyes, not only at him, but also the getaway car, putting all of them in danger of being identified. But in the back he could just climb over the short brick wall without as many eyes looking down at them. Jones did as requested, making sure that he didn't drive erratically and attract attention to the car. Recker ran toward the back of the cemetery and easily climbed over the wall. As his feet hit the ground, his gun still in hand and ready to fire in case of police. Luckily, there was nobody else back there, not even anybody walking through. Recker waited a few seconds until he saw Jones pulling up, Mia safe and sound in the back seat. She opened the back door for him as Recker quickly jumped in and sat next to her.

"Just drive like nothing happened," Recker stated. "We'll stick out like a sore thumb if we speed out of here."

Jones drove back out of the alley, slowly passing by the front of the cemetery. The three of them took a look, noticing an increasing crowd that started pouring through the front gate. Police weren't there yet, but they did detect the sound of a siren that appeared to be coming closer. Jones kept driving, a feeling of relief coming over him as he drove away.

"Once we get back to the office, I'll start to monitor the situation and see what leads they have," Jones said.

"I think I need a vacation," Mia joked, not used to as much excitement as she had experience over the past couple days.

Mia looked at Recker, so thankful for him coming after her. The feelings she had for him only intensified as she stared into his eyes, even though she knew it would never be reciprocated. She put her hand on the side of his cheek and rubbed her thumb against it as she looked at him.

"Thank you," she told him, leaning in and gently kissing him on the lips.

Recker didn't pull away even though he knew he should. After a few seconds, they mutually parted lips and Mia inched over closer to him, giving him a warm embrace as she buried her head into his chest. Recker knew it was a bad idea and simply looked down at the top of her head, leaving his hands free in the air, not wanting to caress her. But as he looked at her, he realized that this would probably be the only chance he ever had, or would permit himself to have, to be with her. He finally relented and dropped his arms, putting them around her back and holding her tightly.

Even though they were caught up in an embrace at the moment, the situation at the cemetery only reinforced what Recker believed to be true. If they were together, she'd always be a target. Though these thugs didn't know the connection between them, it was proof in his mind that it was a situation that they'd have to replay multiple times if it was known of their relationship. Mia would be used as bait to get to him. They hugged for about five minutes before finally separating. They gazed into each other's eyes for another minute, each knowing it was never going any further than what just happened. Mia was actually surprised at the amount of affection that he returned to her. But she could tell by his eyes that he was a man conflicted and she probably just caught him in a weak moment of his after the excitement of the gun battle.

Recker was a man conflicted. Though there was nothing he wanted more at the moment than to keep her in his arms, he couldn't allow himself that pleasure. Holding each other the way they just were was an intoxicating feeling, but he had to restrain himself from giving Mia the wrong impression. For her safety, he needed to keep a distance between them. He looked out the window as they drove over the bridge back into Pennsylvania, and for the second time in as many days, started to wish for a different life, a life that he could never have.

3 CHAPTER PREVIEW

Please enjoy a 3 chapter preview of the next book in The Silencer Series, Blowback.

15

CHAPTER 1

L angley, Virginia—A meeting had been called to discuss the killing of one of their agents, Agent 17. The Director of National Intelligence, as well as CIA Director Roberts had grown very concerned at the agency's lack of progress in finding 17's killer in the past three months. Though it had been swept under the rug in the public's eye, with 17's cover alias intact, the agency's hierarchy was starting to demand some answers. Attending the meeting were Director Roberts, his top aide, Deputy Director Tomlinson, as well as Executive Director Manning, who was in charge of the day-to-day activities of the agency. They were already in conference when Deputy Director Caldwell, who was in charge of operations and collecting foreign intelligence, came walking in. With him, was Sam Davenport, who was in charge of the Centurion Project. Roberts wasted little time in starting the questions as soon as the two visitors were seated.

"You two know why this meeting was called, right?" Roberts asked.

"Yes, sir. The death of Agent 17," Davenport said.

"I'm getting almost daily queries from the DNI as to why we still have not apprehended somebody in his death. He's killed in broad daylight, in a public airport, and three months later here we are sitting on our hands with no answers. What exactly is being done about this and why has it gotten to this point?"

Caldwell and Davenport looked at each other, unsure who should answer. Finally, Caldwell said. "As far as we can tell, there's been no international chatter indicating someone was coming for him or any type of backlash for any work he's done overseas."

"Nothing at all?"

"We've checked all our sources in every country he's been in, every assignment, but there's nothing to suggest it's an outside source."

"Outside source. Why do you phrase it like that?" Roberts said.

Caldwell looked at Davenport, expecting him to take over from there. Davenport cleared his throat and began talking. "We've come to believe it's some type of personal matter."

"Personal matter. Such as?"

"We're still digging into it."

"You're gonna have to give me something better, Sam,"

Roberts said. "You obviously have some type of information leading you in that direction."

"It's more theory on our part right now than actual facts."

"OK. Explain how you got there."

"As Director Caldwell said, we've checked every single assignment 17's been on, and there are no red flags, no anomalies, except for one. And it was internal."

"Internal?" Executive Director Manning asked. "You mean somebody who works for us."

"Well, worked. But yeah, that's what we think," Davenport said.

Manning looked less than convinced. "OK. So why?"

"Three years ago, 17 was part of a group of agents that participated in the elimination of one of our Centurion agents in London."

"What were the circumstances?" Roberts said, locking his fingers together as he prepared to listen.

Davenport opened one of the file folders he'd brought with him and took out papers relating to the case, passing them across the table to each man in the room. There were three sheets of paper stapled together, with information about the assignment, Recker's picture, and his bio.

"John Smith was the alias he used while with us. He was a Centurion operative who'd grown tired of his role with the agency and spilled classified information to his girlfriend at the time," Davenport said.

"It says here he was ambushed in London, but somehow survived the attack," Manning said.

"That's right. He was shot, but he killed three of our

agents in the process, and wound up in a hospital. Once we got word he was there, and we arrived, he was gone."

"And you never found him again?"

"He disappeared. We didn't get another hit on him until six months later when he booked a plane ticket to Orlando, Florida."

"For what purpose?" Roberts looked confused.

"That was where his girlfriend lived and was killed," Davenport said.

"And why was she taken out? The information in this report seems sketchy and doesn't really say much."

"Smith had gone to her and told her about his role in Centurion. We thought it was a security risk."

Roberts investigative tail was up as he started grilling for answers. "Why? How do you know? And how do you know he dispensed information to her? Did you have him bugged, tailed, receive a tip, what?"

"No, Smith told us."

"He told you? He just flat out came into your office and told you?"

"Well, he said he was weary of his job and wanted to leave," Davenport said, trawling his memory. "In the course of our discussion, he indicated he had told his girlfriend certain aspects of his employment. Centurion is a top secret black ops project and cannot be revealed to anyone in any sort of fashion. So, we concluded he was becoming unstable and his girlfriend was a non-essential risk we couldn't tolerate."

Roberts held Davenport's eye for a moment. "So, you

wouldn't have actually had any such information had he not walked into your office and revealed it, correct?"

"Correct."

"Now does it seem logical a man would do that if he was some sort of risk?"

"We didn't feel it was a risk worth taking."

"And how does 17 play into this?"

"17 was the agent who killed Smith's girlfriend," Davenport said as he wiped his face, a sheen of sweat forming on his forehead.

"And you think now, after all this time, Smith came back and killed him for revenge?" Manning said.

"While we have no proof at the moment, it's a working theory we're pursuing right now, yes."

"So, he just dropped out of sight for six months after London," Roberts said. "Then he popped up on the radar with a plane ticket to Florida. What happened there?"

"He never got off the plane."

"So, he probably creates a ruse to get all the attention down there while he moves in a different direction."

"We believe so."

"And Smith knows 17 killed his girlfriend because..." Manning said.

"Smith called his girlfriend to warn her but 17 answered the phone and they had a brief discussion," Davenport said, squirming in his seat.

"This sounds like it came right out of a movie or something," Roberts said. "Do you have Smith's file on you?"

"Not on me, no."

"Jeff, pull up his file."

"No problem," Manning said, typing into his laptop.

The men continued discussing the specifics of the two cases and threw some more theories into the air for a few more minutes until Manning pulled up Smith's file.

"Coming on the big screen now," Manning said.

They turned their heads to look at the monitor on the wall, a big seventy inch screen displaying Smith's personal information, as well as his Centurion assignments. They made several comments in passing as they perused the information before coming to a final conclusion after they finished.

"Looks as close to a perfect record as you can get," Roberts said. "What made you think he was a risk?"

"Just a feeling and from what he had said to me already," Davenport said.

Roberts sighed as he looked down at the desk and wiped his face with his hand, obviously distraught at what was going on.

"This is a complete mess," the director said. "So, we don't know for sure this is the work of Smith. We're just assuming it is."

"Correct," Davenport said.

"And there's no video surveillance from the airport, surrounding areas, roadways, highways, nothing to implicate him either."

"No, but that would give further credence to the theory that it's him. He'd know how to avoid all those things."

"Can I ask why I'm just hearing about this London thing three years later?" Roberts said. "Why wasn't I informed of this when it happened? Jeff, were you aware of this?"

"I was not," Manning said.

"So, who was informed of this plan, Sam?"

"I informed Director Caldwell of our intentions before it was carried out and got his approval," Davenport said. He could feel the damp patch of sweat on his back growing with every minute.

"Dean?"

"I was informed of the general circumstances, but did not review the situation in depth. I relied on the information I was given and gave the green light," Caldwell said.

"And what information was that?" Roberts asked.

"That one of our agents had revealed sensitive information to a civilian and approval was asked for to eliminate that agent along with the civilian he had contact with."

Everyone was silent for a minute as Roberts put his elbow on the table and rubbed his forehead as he looked down at the information Davenport had passed around. There was no doubt the director was obviously displeased at how the situation had been handled. After reading a few paragraphs of text, Roberts finally spoke up again.

"I'm a little bit perplexed, and perturbed, at how this entire situation has not crossed my desk before now," he said. "An agent with a near perfect record was terminated, or attempted as such, along with a United States civilian killed, within our country's borders no less, and I'm just hearing about this three years later. Jeff, how is this possible?"

"I can't say, sir. I wasn't informed of it either," Manning said.

"Sam, can you explain why this didn't go up the chain of command?"

"I asked for permission from Director Caldwell and got it. I figured it was a Centurion issue, and it was handled. Nothing else needed to be said about it," Davenport said.

"For the record, the killing of a civilian within our borders is not a pressing issue that needed to be handled immediately. At least not one who doesn't appear to be much of a threat or flight risk, as this woman was," Roberts said. "I'll give you an agent who's as skilled and lethal as Smith is, maybe there isn't time to go up the ladder. But the woman, that's gotta go across my desk. One hundred percent of the time. Understood?"

"Perfectly, sir."

"Good. Because if you had done so to begin with, I would not have authorized such an action based on the information you've acquired, which is flimsy at best."

"Understood."

"Regardless, it doesn't change the circumstances of whether Smith is responsible for 17's death," Manning said.

"Do we have any idea where Smith may be now?" Roberts said.

"Well, we believe that due to the Orlando plane ticket, he's somewhere in the United States," Davenport said. "Probably on the east coast."

Roberts put his hands together and put them over his

eyes and nose as he shook his head, looking like he had a migraine coming on.

"OK, well, regardless of my feelings of what's already gone down, we need to start making some hay on this," Roberts said. "Sam, you're in charge of Centurion, it's your project, it's your men, you find where Smith is. I want you to put resources into it immediately. You'll report directly to Jeff on this and keep him updated every day on your progress, or lack thereof."

"Yes, sir."

"Once you find his location, you're to sit tight on it and bring it to my desk, is that clear?"

"Perfectly."

"If Smith's our man, and he's the one who killed 17, it's not likely he's gonna go down without a fight. We cannot afford to make a bigger mess on top of the one you've already created." Roberts said, pointedly looking around at the other men in the room.

"Can I ask another question?" Manning said. "What's the status of everyone else who was involved in the London operation?"

"In what way?" Davenport asked.

"Well are they alive, dead, what?"

"Well, the three agents who attempted to kill Smith are dead."

"Killed at the scene while trying to terminate him?"

"Correct?"

"Who else?"

"Smith's handler was in London at the time, and there

was another agent who was at the girlfriend's house in Florida."

"And they're still alive?" Manning said.

"Yes."

"Hmm."

"What are you thinking, Jeff?" Roberts asked.

"Seems kind of strange. If Smith was out for revenge, don't you think he'd take everyone out, not just one?"

"Maybe the one's all he knew."

"An agent's handler is a personal connection. If he was that pissed, wouldn't you think he'd be at the top of the list?" Manning asked. "I mean, Smith would probably know how or where he could take him out if he wanted."

"The other issue is how Smith would have found out where 17 is located," Roberts said. "He didn't hit him overseas, he hit him where he lives. Somebody got him the information."

"We've checked our infrastructure and we've had no data breaches in regard to his file," Davenport said. "And he's got nobody else in the agency to turn to. We've checked to make sure nobody's made contact with him, and from what we can tell, nobody has. We've even kept tabs on his mentor who's now retired, and they've never met or made contact since all this went down."

"Well right now we're looking like world class buffoons, including me since I wasn't aware of any of this, so you better get the situation under control."

"We will. I would suggest one small thing if I could."

"Which is?"

"If we get a hit on him somewhere, I believe we should

take him out immediately," Davenport said. "He's too dangerous to not act right away."

"Sam, you've already bungled one operation, don't make it two." Roberts' warning was clear. "You make a move without clearing it with Jeff or myself and you will pay for it, am I making myself clear?"

"You are."

"It's also very rare for a man, even one as skilled and talented as Smith is, to just vanish without a trace. There's always a bread crumb somewhere. We need to find it. You don't disappear without help. Someone out there knows something. Find them."

16

CHAPTER 2

Recker strolled into the office a little past nine in the morning, ready to begin work on a new case. He finished his previous assignment the day before by disposing of a man who had planned on murdering his wife for insurance money. Though Recker would have preferred doing away with the man permanently, Jones persuaded him to just temporarily disable the perpetrator until police arrived. Recker left enough evidence behind that Jones had discovered which should have been enough to convict the man, without the need for further violence. As soon as Recker walked in, he noticed Jones seemed to be working rather hard, swiveling from one computer to another almost seamlessly.

"Anything on the horizon?" Recker said.

"A few promising prospects," Jones said. "Probably will take another day or two to flesh them out more until we can take action on them."

"Vacation day today then?"

"Hardly."

"Looks like you're typing away hot and heavy for something that's not imminent."

"There's something which requires immediate attention, just not regarding us," Jones said. "Well, it involves us, more specifically you, but not an upcoming case."

"Did you just speak English?"

"What I'm trying to tell you is something popped up on my Recker Radar."

"Recker Radar? Is that actually a thing?"

"It's what I named my government surveillance software program involving you."

"Oh. Interesting," Recker said. "So, you're telling me my name resurfaced somewhere?"

"It did. Approximately three weeks ago there appears to have been a high-level meeting among several high-ranking CIA officers and directors."

"So? It's common you know. It happens all the time."

"Yes, but just before the meeting, I got a hit on a memo with your John Smith alias. It came from someone named Sam Davenport and was sent to Executive Director Manning and the date was two days before that meeting."

"Was Davenport there?" Recker asked, finally concerned.

"He was as far as I can tell. That's one of the issues I was having as I cannot place exactly what this Davenport's role in the agency is."

"He's in charge of the Centurion Project."

"Then you know him?"

"I do. He's the one I initially talked to about leaving the agency. Who else was at this meeting?"

"I've confirmed Director Roberts and Deputy Director Caldwell so far. There may be more," Jones said.

"Let me see the initial memo and anything else you have."

Recker pulled up a chair next to Jones and anxiously waited for him to pull up the information. It was the first time Jones had seen a concerned look on Recker's face after informing him of a possible breach. Recker had always said he wouldn't really be worried about anyone looking for him unless it was the CIA coming. He knew they were the only ones who really had the capabilities of finding him. And if they really were looking for him, Recker knew it was only a matter of time before they found him. Jones finally pulled up the first memo and let Recker read it for himself.

To: Executive Director Manning
From: Sam Davenport

Per your request, we still have no leads into 17's death. We believe it likely to be someone with a personal connection to his past. We have several theories, though nothing concrete. We are looking into the possibility of whether it is related to a job he did that involved a former agent of ours, John Smith. I'll keep you updated.

. . .

Sam

Recker quietly sat there reading the memo, analyzing it, studying it to see if there were any hidden meanings behind any of the words as they sometimes liked to do.

"Anything else?" Recker asked after reading the memo several times.

"Yeah."

Jones brought up another memo, somewhat overlapping the first one on the screen. Recker's eyes were glued to the monitor as he began reading.

To: Sam Davenport
    From: Executive Director Manning

We need further clarification on what's being done at the moment. Director Roberts is calling every day looking for answers and he's getting impatient at the lack of progress. He's called a meeting for this Wednesday at 10am with you, Director Caldwell, and myself. Bring your files and what you have on this Smith and be prepared to explain your plans going forward.

Executive Director Manning

.   .   .

After reading it five times, Recker leaned back in his chair, while still staring at the screen. He put his fingers over his mouth and rubbed his lips as he analyzed the memo. By his mannerisms, Jones detected something was bothering Recker.

"What is it?" Jones said. "It looks as though something's got your attention."

"I'm not sure. It's the way the second memo is worded."

"I didn't notice anything strange or out of the ordinary."

"It's the way Manning identifies me," Recker said. "He called me this Smith."

"And the significance is?"

"Well, in the grand scheme of things, I guess it doesn't make a bit of difference. But on a personal level, I always wondered just how far up the order to kill me went."

"And this helps in that?" Jones asked.

"Well, from the sound of it, it doesn't seem like Manning even knew my name."

"How can you be certain?"

"Well, he called me this Smith. It sounds like he didn't know me. Think about it, anytime a person ever says this in front of someone's name, it indicates a lack of familiarity of the subject. If he knew me, he'd just say Smith, not this Smith."

"Very astute observation, Michael."

"Which probably means the order came either from Davenport or Director Caldwell and didn't go any further up."

"Does that help us somehow?"

"If they're looking for us, doesn't help us a bit," Recker said. "But for my own peace of mind, it helps answer a question I always wondered about."

"How reassuring," Jones said.

"When was all this?"

"Looks like the meeting took place a few weeks ago. The memos aren't dated but that would place them approximately two or three days before I assume. Why would they bother with memos at all? Aren't they all located in the same building?"

"No," Recker said. "Centurion headquarters are in New York. Most black ops programs are located somewhere other than Virginia to try to operate in secrecy. Everyone knows where the CIA building in Virginia is, but it's easier to come and go without prying eyes in a completely different area. Especially a high-volume city such as New York where it's easier to blend in. Rent an office building, register a fictitious name and you're up in business."

"So, what do you propose we do about this?"

"Nothing to do yet until they show up. Just keep going about our day like normal and monitor it best we can."

"You seem pretty sure they will be here."

"Part of me has always known I couldn't run from them forever. It's the way this stuff goes. You knew it too. I guess my stunt down there in Ohio just put me back in the forefront," Recker said.

"There's always packing up and leaving."

Recker grimaced, not really keen on the idea. "We've

put down roots here, made connections, friends... I don't know if it's in the cards now."

"Roots can be replanted, new connections made, and the only friend we've made here is Mia," Jones said.

"Tyrell too. Besides, I don't plan on running forever."

"So, what, you're just going to bunker down and fight like you're the last man at the Alamo?"

"Either way, this doesn't affect you. They won't find a connection between us. Whenever they find out I'm here, it'd be best if we don't get too close for a while."

"Anything that affects you, affects me," Jones said. "I can't do this on my own, and if you're gone, it would mean I have to find, train, and trust a brand-new person."

"You did it once. You can do it again."

Jones grumbled, not liking the situation one bit. "How much time do you think we have?"

"Depends. The quick version... probably a week or so. If it takes a while... few weeks, couple months at the latest."

"I suppose we both knew this would happen, eventually. I just hoped it wouldn't be for a few more years."

"Probably would have been if I hadn't taken 17 out. It would have put me back on the radar. They're looking for connections and I'm probably the only one who fits."

"Well I suppose the good news is we've got advance warning."

"I'll probably have to get word to Mia to let her know I'll be scarce for a while," Recker said.

Jones started squirming in his seat upon hearing her name, not wanting to reveal he was supposed to be meeting her for lunch. Even though Recker and Mia had a few tender moments after their little escapade in New Jersey a few months before, neither one pursued anything more serious upon their return back home. It'd actually been about two weeks since Recker had heard from Mia, which was highly unusual, considering she used to call or text him at least every other day. Jones played off his concerns by telling his partner he'd been hacking into hospital records periodically and checking Mia's time sheets. He kept telling Recker she was having a heavy workload, even working days off and overtime, which was why he hadn't heard from her much. It was an answer that satisfied Recker for the time being.

Jones was not about to be the one to inform Recker that the reason he hadn't heard from Mia was because she started dating someone else. Even though she had every right to find someone, and her and Recker weren't together, Jones still knew how Recker felt about her. He wasn't sure exactly how Recker would take the news. Maybe he'd be fine. Maybe he'd be angry. Maybe he'd get depressed. Maybe he'd be all those things wrapped up in one package. But Jones wasn't going to be the one to tell him about it. Since Recker and Mia were never together, there was no reason he should've objected to a new relationship of hers, but his feelings for her were a fickle business. Sometimes they changed with the weather and sometimes for what seemed like no reason at all. Maybe it was because Jones knew Recker really felt more for Mia than just being friends and didn't want to be the one who disappointed him, even though Recker himself said things couldn't go further with her. But what he said and what he would actually feel when she actually did move on were two different things.

The only reason Jones even agreed to meet Mia for lunch at all was because she was really persistent. She was good at it. She never did take no for an answer very well. She contacted Jones almost a week ago to ask if he could meet her for lunch. She wanted to talk to him about her new boyfriend and how to tell Recker about it, if at all. One thing Jones never imagined being when he started up this operation, was the middleman in a love triangle. He reluctantly agreed to meet Mia, mostly because he needed for Recker not to go off the deep end when he found out, and he hoped by talking with her, they could figure out the best way to break it to him.

Once noon came around, Jones started wrapping up his work on the computer. Recker was on one of the other computer stations, trying to figure out his CIA issue. His attention was diverted when he saw Jones stand, appearing like he was going out somewhere. It was pretty unusual behavior for him. Though Jones every now and then would go out for lunch, he never did when there was what appeared to be an urgent situation. And Recker figured this CIA issue could be classified as an urgent situation. Jones usually would work right through lunch and keep himself glued to his chair. So, him leaving right about now struck a chord with Recker.

"Where are you going?" Recker said.

"I have a prior engagement I have to attend."

"An engagement? What, like a party or something?"

"No," Jones said, trying to think of something else to tell him.

"Uh... then where are you going?"

"I'm meeting a contact."

"A contact? Like who?"

"Well, I can't tell you."

"Why?"

"I don't know his name," Jones said, caught in a lie.

"This is highly unusual for you, don't you think? It's usually me meeting contacts."

"Desperate times call for desperate measures."

"I didn't realize we were in desperate times," Recker said.

"Well, alarming times, how's that?"

"You want me to come along for backup?"

"No. Won't be necessary."

"You want me to monitor things from here?"

"No, I'll be fine," Jones said.

"You're being awfully cloak and dagger about this thing."

"As you know, some things have to be kept close to the vest."

"Where'd you find this contact?"

"I can't say. I'll fill you in when I get back."

"Do I have to worry? Dangerous perhaps?"

"No danger involved. It's just an exchange of information," Jones said, hoping it would be enough to quiet Recker down.

Though he wasn't really satisfied with that answer, or

any of the other ones that Jones had said, Recker stopped with the questions. He realized that Jones wasn't going to tell him anything useful, so he figured it was best to just let him go. Besides, with the CIA starting to breathe down his neck, Recker didn't have time to worry about more trivial things. If Jones really needed his help, he would've asked.

When Jones got to the restaurant, Mia was already sitting and waiting. Upon seeing her, the Professor looked at his watch and hurried over to her table. Mia gave him a big smile, then stood to give him a warm hug. She had already ordered drinks for the two of them so they took their seats to look at the menu.

"Thanks for coming," Mia said.

"Sorry I'm late." Jones checked his watch. "I got caught up with things, then I hit traffic, then..."

"David, it's OK. I'm just glad you're here."

Jones lifted his drink and looked at the top of it.

"Sweetened iced tea, just the way you like it."

"You know me so well."

"Yeah, it's nice the two of us getting together like this. We should do it more often."

"Yes, I don't remember the last time we did this," Jones said.

"David, we've never done this."

"Oh, nonsense. We've had lunch together plenty of times."

"Yeah, at my apartment, or with you, me, and Mike. But never just us, out somewhere. It's kind of nice. Different."

"It is. So, should we get to the basis of this meeting?" Jones asked.

"Meeting? You make this sound so formal. Can't two friends just sit and have lunch together?"

"Indeed, they can. Our relationship, however, has never been predicated upon lunch dates or social gatherings. You indicated that you wanted advice on your situation with Michael, did you not?"

"Well, yeah."

"Well then, why beat around the bush, or dance around the subject, or pretend it's for some other reason? Friends talk about other friends, right?"

"OK," Mia said, unsure how to proceed.

She stuttered for a minute and started to say something, though no words came out of her mouth. She was very uneasy and nervous talking about the subject at all. But she knew it was better to talk it over with someone else first before approaching Recker with it. And since the only mutual friend they had was Jones, he was the only candidate for the job. Jones could see she was struggling to start the conversation, but he wasn't exactly an expert in love or relationships, so he had no idea how to help her or draw out her feelings on the matter.

"So, you're obviously aware of, uh, my... feelings for Mike," she said, stammering and taking a deep breath as if she was having a panic attack.

"Mia, you don't have to go into any kind of deep explanation of personal emotions," Jones said, trying to calm her down before she passed out or something. "I'm well aware you and Mike have an emotional attachment of sorts, but due to his... career, it is not possible to further explore those feelings you have for each other."

"OK, well, a few weeks ago I met someone."

"And?"

"Well, we went on a few dates and he now wants to date exclusively," Mia said calmly, not really believing she was saying the words.

"And your feelings are?"

"I think I might want to."

"Excellent. I think it's a fabulous idea," Jones said, without hesitation.

"You do?"

"Absolutely. You and Mike have never progressed beyond friends and I think it's time you moved on. You deserve it."

"But you don't even know who it is or what he does or anything," Mia said.

"Well who is he?"

"His name's Josh and he's a lawyer."

"Oh," Jones said, cracking a face.

"Well you don't have to say it like that. He's a really nice guy. He's not like a sleazy lawyer or anything."

"What kind is he?"

"He's a personal injury lawyer," she said. "You know, helps people who are hurt at work and the like."

"And people who spill coffee on themselves at restaurants then sue the restaurant I suppose?"

"No! At least I don't think so. Well, I dunno, but he's a really nice guy."

"Makes good money? Treats you right?"

"Yes. Well, the treating me right part. So far anyway. I'm not sure about the money. I haven't asked about his bank account, but he has his own house and a nice car so I assume he's doing all right."

"As I said, if you're happy, you have my blessings. Are you having doubts about this arrangement?"

"No. I think I want to."

"Why does it sound like you're having misgivings then?" Jones asked.

"I don't know. I guess part of me has always just been waiting for Mike to come riding in on the white horse and take me away."

"Mia, Mike doesn't own a white horse. And continually waiting for something that in all likelihood will not happen is not going to help either of you move on, especially you."

"I know." She looked downcast as she fiddled with her thumbs.

"If you really have feelings for this Josh, and you think it could possibly lead somewhere you want, then you should try to make it work."

"Should I tell Mike or no?" Mia said.

"You absolutely should tell Mike."

"You wouldn't want to kind of casually mention it to him somehow, would you?"

Jones had taken a sip of his drink, almost spitting it out at her reference. He wiped his mouth with a napkin before answering. "No. No, I would not. I'm here for advice counseling and that is all. I'm not doing the dirty work for you."

"How do you think he'll take it?"

"Well, it sort of depends on what kind of mood he's in. There's really no way of telling in advance. If he takes it well, maybe he'll wish you well and just go back to work like it's no big deal," Jones said.

"And if he takes it badly?"

"Maybe he'll just wish you well then go back to work and shoot somebody."

17

CHAPTER 3

When Jones got back to the office after his luncheon with Mia, he noticed Recker was in the same spot as when he left. Jones wondered if he even moved at all in the couple hours he'd been gone. Recker was staring hard at the computer, barely even paying any attention to Jones since he walked in.

"Have you even moved from that spot since I left?" Jones said.

Recker gave him a quick glance before returning his eyes back to the screen. "There's a lot going on."

"I don't think I've ever seen you so concerned about something before."

"I told you I would never worry until the CIA came looking. This is why."

"Just the same. I think I preferred your carefree attitude."

"So how was your meeting?" Recker asked.

"Uh... good."

"So, what are you trying to hide from me?"

"What? Hide from you?" Jones asked, trying to laugh it off. "What are you talking about?"

"Well, in all the time we've known each other, you've never been so secretive before. Now suddenly you're going off, not telling me where you're going, who you're meeting, seems kind of fishy."

"I'm just not at liberty to reveal their name."

"What was it about?"

"Just a... case."

"A case we're not on," Recker said. "Considering I finished the last one yesterday."

"Well, about the CIA problem."

"And you don't think it's worth sharing?"

Recker could tell Jones was just saying whatever popped into his mind. If it was really about a case, Jones would've just come out and said what it was about. He wouldn't have danced around the subject like he was doing. And if it was really about the CIA, it wasn't something Jones would've kept to himself. So, if it wasn't about a case, or the CIA, then it must've been something personal. Either for Recker or for Jones. With a few suspicions as to what it might've been about, Recker lobbed a few more questions at his friend, just to see how he'd handle them. After a short give and take, Recker thought he might've figured it out. At least partially.

"Is this about Mia?" Recker asked.

"What? Mia? Why would it be about Mia?" Jones asked incredulously.

"Because I haven't heard from her in a week, you're being ultra secretive, sounds like you two are planning something."

"Don't be ridiculous. What on earth would we be planning?"

"That's a good question. Why don't you answer it?"

"I can't."

"Do I have to call Mia and ask her?"

Jones suddenly looked much more pleasant. "Yes. Yes, I think you should do that."

"If I can ever get her on the phone," Recker said.

Though Jones kept buttoned up and steadfastly refused to confirm anything else, he didn't deny whatever he was hiding had something to do with Mia. For Recker it was basically a confirmation it was true. Recker grabbed his phone and made another call to Mia, once again going to voicemail. This time, he left a message.

"I guess now I know how it feels," Recker said.

"What's that?"

"Trying to call someone repeatedly and not getting an answer. I guess now I know how she's felt these past couple years when she called and I didn't answer."

"Oh. Well, turnabout is fair play as they say," Jones said.

Not having to answer any more questions, Jones sat again and got back to work. With nothing new on the CIA front, he pulled up some of the cases he'd been keeping an eye on lately. As he was working, Recker continued his CIA search, trying to glean any new information he could. After about thirty minutes, Jones made a couple of muffled sounds which distracted Recker. Since the Professor didn't say anything to him, Recker played it off and kept going about his own business. A few minutes later, Jones made the same type of noises, drawing Recker's attention again. He put his elbow on the table and rested his head on his hand staring at his partner, waiting for an explanation of his troubles. Jones didn't even seem to realize what he was doing and never took his eyes off his screen. A few more minutes went by with Recker staring and he finally got tired of waiting for an explanation.

"So, do you wanna spill it?"

Recker's voice finally broke Jones' concentration, and he looked over at his partner. "Hmm?"

"Do you wanna share what's so fascinating about whatever it is you're looking at?"

"I wish it was fascinating," Jones said. "It's more like... disturbing."

"Well, are you going to share?"

"Oh. It's one of the cases I've been monitoring. To be honest, it's one I hoped would just somehow magically go away without us having to get involved. Sadly, it doesn't seem to be the case."

"What's the trouble?"

"It's um..." Jones hesitated, rubbing his head as he thought of the best way to explain it.

Recker didn't recall a case in which Jones had trouble stating the issue before. It was his first tip-off it might be something big. "Just say it."

"Well, it's actually two people I've been keeping an eye

on. I first caught wind of a text message one of them sent to the other about... children," Jones said, struggling to get the words out.

"Children? What do you mean, children? What about them?"

"One of them is a convicted child sex offender."

"What's the message say?" Recker asked.

"Well, apparently one of them has been watching an elementary school and has his eyes on a couple of kids. Some of the language they use is... well, I just can't repeat it. Not when thinking about kids. Here, you look at it."

Jones moved his chair over a little so Recker could come in and take a look at what he was seeing. Recker read the messages the two men had been sending to each other regarding the children they were seeking out. Recker had seen and heard a lot of things, and not much really bothered him. But reading what these two men were planning on doing to some small children really disgusted him.

"Who are these creeps?" Recker asked.

"Reed Laine and Sidney Bowman."

"Both convicted sex offenders?"

"Only Laine is. He is not allowed to be anywhere near a school. Bowman on the other hand, does not appear to have any kind of criminal record," Jones said, still clearly bothered by what he had picked up on.

"How do these two jerks know each other?"

"That I do not know off-hand. It appears the two somehow befriended each other somewhere along the line over the years. Maybe online, maybe in a chat room, maybe on a message board, maybe somewhere on the dark web, who knows? I do know they weren't childhood friends. They grew up in different areas, different schools, never worked together. So, my best guess is they hooked up online somewhere due to their fascination with... the kids. That seems to be the tie binding them together."

"Wonderful. Anything concrete on the time and place of what they're planning?"

"Nothing definitive as of yet."

Recker took a few steps back then walked over to his gun cabinet. He selected his two weapons, his primary and backup, as per his usual. As he closed the cabinet, he looked over at Jones, who appeared to be deep in thought. Jones was kind of staring away from the computer toward the wall, not seeming to be looking at anything in particular.

"What is it?" Recker asked.

"I was just thinking if maybe it'd be a good idea if we kept a low profile for a while."

"You mean take a vacation?"

"No. Just work more in the shadows. Relay our information to the authorities, let them handle things," Jones said. "Kind of stay quiet."

"You want us to sit on our hands while these two jerks are out there molesting kids?"

"No. Not at all. We can forward what we have to the police and let them take over the investigation."

"Why?"

"Well, with the CIA looking into your whereabouts

again, I just think it may be wise to stay in the background until things blow over a little."

"David, I'm not someone who just sits on my hands very well."

"I'm aware."

"Besides, what can the police do?"

"Monitor their behavior and such."

"Yeah, monitor their behavior after they've already committed some heinous act some poor kid will never emotionally recover from," Recker said.

"I'm not saying we should do nothing."

"I know. You're just saying to let someone else do the dirty work."

"I'm just worried. If something happens, it may put you even more in the spotlight. A spotlight we don't need at the moment," Jones said. "Any type of publicity The Silencer gets at this moment may be something which draws the CIA closer to our doorstep. To your doorstep."

"You can't live in fear, waiting, wondering, hoping something doesn't happen."

"I'm not saying we should be living in fear, I'm just wanting to exercise some caution."

"Listen, I hear you and I understand your concern. But it doesn't really change anything. Do you really wanna put this in the hands of the police and take chances on the lives of children? What if the police can't act on the information you give them? Which is likely. What if they have too much on their plate and they don't get to these creeps in time? You're leaving a lot to chance."

"I know."

"And if this was some run-of-the-mill nut job and innocent children weren't at play, then maybe I'd agree with you. But I won't stand by and let children be targets. I didn't sign up for this to stand on the sidelines."

Jones nodded, completely understanding Recker's position, and actually agreeing with it. Even though he suggested caution, Jones knew his partner was right on point with his arguments and he really had no winning argument against them. Now that they were in agreement that they shouldn't do anything different than usual, Recker went back to the computer to get more information.

"Where am I gonna find these clowns?" Recker asked.

"Reed Laine lives on Washington Street and Sidney Bowman lives on Ashford."

"Do we know what school they're targeting."

"They didn't say. But, judging from where they live and the approximately to the closest school, I can take a guess," Jones said.

Recker took a final look at their addresses to memorize it before heading out to find them. He usually could commit everything to memory, but asked Jones to send him the information just in case.

"Send their pictures and whatnot to my phone," Recker said.

"Mike, if I can give some advice, please handle this as quietly as possible."

"Should I leave them tied up in the middle of a room with some porno mags taped to their chests?" he asked sarcastically.

"I'm just saying discretion is sometimes the better part of valor."

"I'll do what has to be done. No more, no less. Just like always."

Recker bid his partner goodbye and left the office to find their targets. Once he exited the office, Jones got a bad feeling about his intentions.

"Just like always. That's the part I'm worried about," Jones muttered.

As Recker drove, Jones forwarded the requested information to his phone. He sent the pictures of the two men, along with their addresses, work information, as well as DMV information on their cars. Everything Recker might possibly need to find the two as quickly as possible, he now had. Considering the two men only lived a few blocks from each other, Recker wouldn't have far to go to find either of them. Recker's first target was Laine, who was the closest. It took Recker about twenty-five minutes to reach the Laine address. Laine lived in a row home in an end unit. There was a small driveway big enough to house one car in the three-story home, though there was no car sitting there. Laine was supposed to be driving a small gray Toyota. Many owners of these homes also parked on the street by the curb due to the lack of space so Recker cruised up and down the street, and even on the connecting streets, just to make sure it wasn't nearby. But it wasn't in sight. Instead of sitting waiting for a while, Recker drove over to the address of Bowman, which was only about five minutes away. He also lived in a similar house, a row home, though his unit was in the middle.

Once Recker found the address, he parked across the street. He saw a light blue Ford belonging to Bowman parked in the driveway. While Laine was single and lived by himself, Bowman was living with his parents, as the house was registered in their names.

While the thought occurred to Recker to just burst through the front door and start blasting away, he didn't want to hurt or injure innocent people, which he assumed Bowman's parents to be. Recker called Jones and asked him to run a quick background check on them just to make sure they were unaware of their son's behavior. Recker would just sit tight until Jones got back to him with the information. He also wasn't sure if the parents were even there at the moment. So, while he preferred not to wait at the moment, he figured it was the best strategy for the time being. After uneventfully sitting there for half an hour, Jones got back to him with the information he had requested.

"As far as I can tell, Bowman's parents are not connected to their son's activity in any way," Jones said.

"They don't know anything about it?"

"Well, they know their son has issues, and it looks like they've tried to get him help with psychiatrists and doctors and the like, but it doesn't appear the apple falls from the tree if you get my meaning."

"So, they don't know he's staking out schools and kids right now," Recker said.

"It wouldn't appear so."

That bit of information confirmed Recker's strategy to wait until he could get Bowman alone. Since the parents didn't seem to be involved, he was going to make sure they weren't hurt in whatever went down. Recker still wasn't sure what he was going to do, but everything going through his mind seemed to have a violent end to it. He knew it wasn't what Jones wanted, but in this case, Recker didn't see another way around it. Maybe Jones was right and they should tread carefully, but with kids involved, Recker just wasn't willing to tap dance around. He'd do what he thought was right and let the chips fall where they may.

Two more hours went by and Recker was starting to get a little antsy. Though he didn't usually get anxious over cases, when kids were involved, and not knowing exactly when the two subjects were planning on putting their plans into motion, he was ready to get moving. Fortunately, he didn't have much longer to wait. He saw the front door open, and a man came out of the house. Recker looked at his phone for confirmation it was Bowman. It was. At first glance, Bowman didn't appear to be a very threatening type of guy. He wasn't big or imposing or tough looking. He was in his mid to late forties, rim glasses, and kind of small at five feet four or five. Seeing him for the first time, you wouldn't expect him to be the type who'd have issues like this. But, as Recker was well aware, most people had secrets hidden away. He watched as Bowman locked the door to the house, walked down the steps then got into his car. As he pulled away and drove down the street, Recker followed him, keeping a safe distance behind him so Bowman wouldn't see he was being followed.

After driving for a few minutes, it became clear where Bowman was going. Once he made a left turn at the traffic light, there was an elementary school dead ahead. Bowman drove up to the edge of school property and parked just alongside the curb. It was recess and most of the kids were outside playing. Recker parked about five car lengths behind his target and just sat there watching him. As he sat there, he called Jones to let him know what was happening.

"Well, looks like we know what's on Bowman's mind," Recker said.

"Which is?"

"He just drove down to the elementary school and parked. He's watching the kids at recess."

"That is alarming, isn't it?"

"There's no use in waiting, is there?"

"We could call the police and have them run him off," Jones said.

"What for? You said he has no record. There's nothing stopping him from being near school grounds."

"I'm just searching for an alternative."

"There are no alternatives," Recker said. "You and I both know what has to be done."

Even though Recker seemed strongly in favor of capital punishment, he wasn't as sure in his own mind. It was part of why he called Jones to begin with. Part of him hoped that Jones had another solution at hand, even though Recker knew there was none. He knew what he had to do. Recker partially opened his car door, ready to unleash his brand of justice, but then thought better of it.

He heard the joyful screaming of the kids playing in the background and it caused Recker to pause. He then shut his door again as he contemplated a better option. Killing Bowman near school property just didn't seem like the right move. There'd be a big commotion, along with a police presence, news cameras and reporters, and a lot of outside noise that Recker didn't think was fair to subject a bunch of young kids to seeing. Recker would have to wait and pick a better spot. As he continued thinking about his plans, his phone rang. It was Jones.

"Yeah?"

"You haven't done anything yet, have you?" Jones asked.

"No. Not yet. Why?"

"Well, as we've noted, Bowman doesn't have any type of record. It appears his family has tried to get him help for his problem."

"So? We already know all that. What's your point?" Recker said.

"My point is, you don't have to do what we both know you're planning on doing."

"I asked you for alternatives earlier. You didn't have any."

"Well, maybe if you just talked to him, let him know you're watching him, that may be enough to scare him off," Jones said.

"You really think so? People like this are sick. You really believe a good talking to is all he needs? What do you think happened when he visited the psychiatrist?" Recker asked.

"Would it hurt?"

"Well it might not hurt, but it sounds like a complete waste of time. Don't forget we got one more guy out there doing who knows what."

"Believe me, I'm well aware of that."

"You really think a little chat is going to do any good?"

"It's worth a try," Jones said.

Recker let out a little grunt, "Fine. But I'm telling you this is a waste of time."

"Noted."

Recker hung up and quickly got out of his car, not wanting to waste any more time. With his guns tucked firmly out of sight inside the belt of his pants, he closed his car door and took a look around to make sure he wasn't being watched or there was nobody nearby who could see any commotion going on. With the coast clear, Recker started walking toward Bowman's car. As he approached it, he could see Bowman was looking at the school playground through a pair of cheap looking binoculars. Seeing that made Recker even angrier and more agitated than he already was. Still unsure what he was going to do or say, Recker was just kind of making things up as he went along. He stopped when he got alongside the driver side window. Bowman didn't even realize he was there at first. Recker knocked on the window to get his attention. Startled, Bowman jumped in his seat a little when he saw the intimidating looking man standing outside his window.

"What do you want?" Bowman asked without rolling the window down.

Recker tilted his head and pointed at his ears, pretending he couldn't quite make out what Bowman was saying. Agitated, Bowman rolled his window down.

"I said, what do you want?"

"Oh, I was just wondering why you were sitting here looking at little kids," Recker said.

"Go away."

Bowman attempted to roll his window back up but Recker prevented him from doing so at first by putting his hands on the edge of the glass. Eventually though, the force of the power window made him lose his grip, and the window rolled all the way up. Rattled, Bowman reached for the ignition and turned the key in an attempt to leave the scene. Obviously, Recker's attempts for a conversation were not off to a good beginning. Though he could've just let Bowman leave since he was obviously rattled and perhaps Recker thwarted his plans, it just wasn't good enough for Recker. He reached around to his back and withdrew one of his guns and turned it around, holding it by the barrel. Recker then took the weapon and slung it to the side of his head as he viciously brought it back down like a backhanded slap, rapping it against the glass as the window shattered. Bowman stopped what he was doing and put his arms up over his head to protect himself from shards of glass cutting into his face. After a few seconds, Bowman put his arms back down, revealing his face once again to the stranger on the outside. Recker once again swung his weapon in a back-handed manner, this time forcefully hitting Bowman across the bridge of his nose, causing his head to violently snap back against the headrest. Recker then moved the gun to his left hand and reached through the window and unleashed a right cross that caused Bowman to slump across the gear lever in the middle console. Recker pulled the lock up on the inside of the door and opened it, pushing Bowman completely into the passenger seat, though half of his body was on the floor of the seat well. With Bowman in a lot of pain and holding his face due to the blood dripping down from his broken nose, Recker took control of the wheel and peeled out of the parking space.

"Who are you? What do you want?" Bowman yelled, though it was somewhat garbled as his hands were covering his mouth from still holding his nose.

"I'm just a concerned citizen," Recker said.

Recker wasn't exactly sure where he was going, figuring something would occur to him as he was driving. Or maybe, he'd see something which would just stick out to him as a good place to go. His phone started ringing again, though he didn't even check to see who it was, assuming it was Jones, and he didn't especially feel like talking to him again at the moment.

"Where are we going?" Bowman asked.

"Just shut up."

"You broke my nose."

Recker kept his eyes on the road, not feeling bothered at all. "I'm heartbroken."

"Why are you doing this to me?"

Recker didn't respond and instead focused on driving. He noticed Bowman starting to move around a little more, like he was about to get off the floor entirely and get in the seat.

"Just stay where you are or I'll break a few more things," Recker said.

He didn't feel the least bit threatened by the man, but Recker didn't want to take chances and have his passenger try something stupid. Having him kneeling on the floor kept him at a more acceptable distance. After a short drive, Recker saw a small shopping center and pulled in, parking near the outside of it, as far away from the stores as possible. It was a small center that had a grocery store, drug store, pizza shop, as well as a few other small establishments.

"Looks like this is where it ends, sonny," Recker said.

Bowman looked worried. "What are you gonna do with me?"

"Well, you and your friend Laine seem to have a little problem with looking at the kids, huh?"

"I don't know what you're talking about."

"Do I look stupid to you?"

"No."

"I've seen the messages you two creeps have sent to each other."

"It was nothing," Bowman said, shrugging his shoulders. "We were just kind of kidding around."

"You don't joke about things like that. Besides, if it was just kidding around, you wouldn't have been at the school where I found you, would you?"

"I was just taking a drive and parked for a few minutes. The kids make me feel good."

"Yeah, I bet they do." Recker felt sick to the stomach at the thought of what kind of 'good' the kids made Bowman feel.

"So, what are you gonna do?" Bowman asked, seeing the gun sitting on the seat between Recker's legs.

"Well, I'm supposed to be having a chat with you to tell you never to do it again but I have a feeling it's gonna be useless. Isn't it?"

"I'll do whatever you want."

"Yeah, I kind of figured you'd say that. Then tomorrow when I'm not around anymore you'll find yourself right back in the same situation."

"No. I swear."

Recker sighed, unsure of the point of having the conversation. He could tell it wasn't going anywhere. And like he said, as soon as he was gone, Bowman would be right back to doing the same thing. He wasn't going to change just because of a conversation with Recker. Recker wasn't sure why he even bothered to listen to Jones and try this method first. It was a complete waste of time. He should've just done what he wanted to do in the beginning. Recker grabbed the Glock from between his legs and pointed it at Bowman. Without thinking or blinking, he fired three rounds into his target's chest, killing the man instantly as his face slumped down onto the seat, his shirt soaked in blood.

He didn't want to stay at the scene very long, so Recker quickly got out of the car and started walking back to his. Luckily it wasn't too far away. It'd give him some time to calm down. Shooting someone was never a good feeling, no matter who it was, though Recker knew taking out someone like that was necessary. As he walked, he reached into his pocket and removed his phone to see who had called him. As he suspected, it was Jones. To pass the time, Recker called him back.

"You need something?" Recker asked.

"I was just calling to see how you were making out."

"Good."

"When you say good, you mean?"

"I mean it's done. Onto the next one."

"You talked with Bowman?" Jones said.

"I did. Didn't do a bit of good."

"Oh. So, what happened?"

"What do you think happened? He's dead," Recker said.

"Oh."

"I did what had to be done."

ABOUT THE AUTHOR

Mike Ryan is a USA Today Bestselling Author. He lives in Pennsylvania with his wife, and four children. He's the author of the bestselling Silencer Series, as well as many others. Visit his website at www.mikeryanbooks.com to find out more about his books, and sign up for his newsletter. You can also interact with Mike via Facebook, and Instagram.

 facebook.com/mikeryanauthor
 instagram.com/mikeryanauthor

ALSO BY MIKE RYAN

Continue reading the next book in The Silencer Series, Blowback.

Other Books:

The Extractor Series

The Cain Series

The Eliminator Series

The Ghost Series

The Brandon Hall Series

The Cari Porter Series

A Dangerous Man

The Last Job

The Crew